Black Love

Black Love,

Volume 1:

Summer's Pleasure

Devonaire Fa'ness

Golden Pen Publications

Cincinnati, Ohio

Golden Pen Publications

Cincinnati, Ohio

This is a work of fiction. Any similarities to real persons or events are purely coincidental.

ISBN: 978-1-7372692-1-2

Cover design by Allen Cartwright of Custom Web Choice

Edited by Derrick Simmons

Foreword

Devonaire Fa'Ness is back with another scintillating tale of reality, passion and restoration!

Ladies, it is a woman's divine nature to love and be loved. Unfortunately, when the act is not reciprocated, many fall into the habit of normalizing dysfunction, desensitizing themselves to the emotional and psychological trauma of a toxic relationship. In doing so, they become complicit in their own unhappiness.

Black Love is a novel that depicts black women and men in positive ways that reflect the beauty of togetherness. It explores the challenging and oftentimes humorous aspects of relationships, from being married and raising a family to dating and fearfully starting over.

The lives and relationships of Brooke, Hanifa, and Michaela will resonate with some and inspire others. Black Love is an emotional intervention that will stimulate your sexual desires and simultaneously restore the image of what love looks like, sounds like, and feels like.

Prologue

I was unsure of the exact time, but I knew it was the wee hours of the morning. Silence and darkness permeated the bedroom. The comfort and warmth of his imposing naked body pressing against mine as we spooned made me feel loved, wanted, and protected.

I felt the rhythm of his heartbeat as his moist lips kissed my back. He was wide awake, and his erect, throbbing nature was smushed against my butt. This was a clear indicator that he wanted some more loving, which I was more than willing to accommodate his desires.

He pumped against my butt, seeking the slightest sign of me acknowledging his request, so I nestled up under him. He pumped again. This time, I nudged back with my butt. All of a sudden, the vibration of his deep voice grazing over my skin caused the hairs on the back of my neck to stand as chills streaked down my spine. Instantly, I became aroused.

His big, manly hand stroked and caressed my leg and butt. He knew just how and where to touch me. He slipped his hand between my thighs, and his fingertip swiped my moist folds. Eyes closed, still pretending to be half-asleep, I casually moved my leg, providing ample room for his hand and fingers to access my secret garden.

His thick fingers gently rubbed my coochie in a circular motion, getting me wet, then his middle finger entered my garden and began finger fucking me in a smooth, rhythmic motion. Being fingered never felt better.

My body quickly warmed up. My pussy responded by getting wetter. He incorporated another finger, adding girth, and my eyes opened as he penetrated deeper, causing a subtle moan to slip from my lips. *Uaahh!* There was no need to pretend, for he knew I was awake.

He moved his fingers faster, causing my moans to become more frequent as I drew closer to climaxing. When he stopped and withdrew his magical fingers, I was disappointed. *Shit!* A few more minutes and I would have exploded. But it was just about to get real. He nudged me to raise my legs, then slid down and lined up his dick so he could enter me from the perfect angle. With my leg raised, I held onto the pillow anticipating the exhilarating sensation of the initial entry. The tip of his dick breached my pearly gates, and my pussy began stretching as he pushed deep inside of me. *Uaahh... yes!* I moaned in delight.

The warmth of his big dick gliding in and out sent flashes of heat racing all over my body. I gyrated in unison with his back-and-forth motion, meeting him stroke for stroke. Within minutes, the pace increased and his breathing became uneven. I knew he was about to cum, so I reached back, caressed his face, and told him how good it felt. I did this while moaning loudly. I was seconds away from climaxing. Yes! Yes! Yes! I moaned feverishly, bracing for the explosion of pleasure ready to erupt.

Five!

Four!

Three!

Two! One...

Chapter 1

(Brook)

Beep... Beep...

Awakened by the blaring sound of the alarm clock going off, I opened my eyes and realized it was all a dream. I reached over on the nightstand and hit the snooze button to quieten the annoying racket. It didn't matter what time I went to sleep, 5:30am always managed to come sooner than I liked. My three-year old daughter, Yasmin, laid beside me. Somehow, she was able to sleep through the entire commotion without a stir.

Although my lover may have been a figment of my imagination, my biological reactions to the perceived sexual stimulation was real, very real. My t-shirt was soaked in sweat, my nipples were hard, and my pussy was extremely wet. I couldn't believe how vivid and surreal the dream felt. The way he touched, kissed, and stroked me with his big dick was just how I liked to be touched. *Stupid alarm clock. You could've at least waited for a sister to get off before going off.* Now, that's what is meant by some one or some thing fucking up a wet dream.

Sexually frustrated, I took a deep breath and exhaled. It was go time, so I got up and shuffled downstairs to the kitchen to turn on the expresso machine, then proceeded with my morning routine. By 6:30am, we were out the door and headed to Ms. Jones', my daycare provider. She was a sweet, elderly woman whose house was close to the school, which was a major convenience considering Atlanta's morning traffic.

I have been the principal at Frederick Douglas Elementary School for the past four years. My district consisted primarily of children from low-income families, and for many, the two meals we provided were essential. Every morning, I greeted the students in front of the main entrance. My secretary, Mrs. Nelly, and I corralled the hyperactive, little kids inside and made sure they ate breakfast. My district primarily consisted of children from low-income families. For many, the two meals we provided were essential.

Mrs. Nelly was the school's self-appointed matriarch and grandmother figure. She'd been there long enough to remember when most of our students' parents attended school there. She was funny and kind, yet stern. At 35 years of age, I was the youngest principal she had worked for. We got along fine, and because of my stylish wardrobe she often referred to me as 'the runway principal'. What can I say? It's a Detroit thang! At 35 years of age, I was the youngest principal Mrs. Nelly worked for, but we got along just fine.

The school year was coming to an end, but not fast enough. It had been one hell of a year for me, and I needed the summer break for my mental and emotional wellbeing. As I sat at my desk staring out the window, my mind drifted off and I began reflecting on how things in my life had gotten to the point they were at.

I was born and raised on the westside of Detroit. The D, as we called it, instilled in me toughness, street smarts, and good, old-fashioned common sense. Growing up, I was a cool chick; I was known for my hazel eyes. I excelled in school, wasn't with the drama, and was obedient to my parents, for the most part. My parents had been together for 35 years, married for 26. They were my living example of what black love was all about. They loved one another. Both worked at the Ford plant, overcame challenges, and raised a family.

Although I loved and respected my parents, by my senior year of high school I knew I wanted more than a factory job. I wanted more for my life than what many of my friends would settle for. I needed to carve out a place in the world just for me, so after graduation I left to attend Clarke University in Atlanta, Georgia.

From the moment I arrived in Atlanta I fell in love with EVERYTHING: the people, restaurants, stores, and the nightlife culture. My dorm mates were two, dope chicks named Hanifa and Michaela. Hanifa was a tall, beautiful, dark-skinned girl from California. Her parents were members of the Black Panthers, so she was raised with a militant mindset and Afrocentric swag like Erykah Badu's. Michaela was from Atlanta; she was a true Georgia peach in every sense of the word. She was a cute, caramel-complected chick with short hair like Toni Braxton, and had a body that could stop rush-hour traffic. She was on the dance team. She also moonlighted as a bottle-girl at several of the city's hottest clubs, which benefitted me and Hanifa because it gave us access to all of Hot-lanta! The three of us clicked from the beginning and formed a sisterhood that persists to this day.

While pursuing a Master's Degree at Georgia Tech, I met Darius, a handsome, brown-skinned man from Atlanta with deep waves. Like most southern men, he was a real charmer. The courtship was exciting. We talked on the phone a lot, went to concerts and out to eat regularly, and had sex all the time. After two years, he proposed and we got married. We purchased a newly built, four bedroom, two-car garage, home in the Piedmont area. Four years later, I got pregnant.

Things between Darius and I began to change during my pregnancy. We didn't spend time together like we did before. I was busy with work and school, and his job as a pharmaceutical representative had him traveling all over the country. What was once charm and affection became chaos and neglect. Arguments became a staple in our home, especially when he started coming in during the wee hours of the morning. I was stressed, to say the least.

Home life improved for a while after Yasmin was born. Darius spoiled her rotten. He spent a lot more time around the house being the version of himself I fell in love with. Unfortunately, his questionable behavior returned, and so did the arguments. It was so bad that at one point we couldn't be around one another for ten minutes without arguing about something.

Our sex life had become non-existent. This was a major concern to me. Like most guys, Darius loves pussy and having his dick sucked. When we did have sex, it felt cold and empty. I felt like he no longer desired me sexually. After a while, I couldn't even get wet for him anymore, so we stopped altogether. I'll admit, I was still carrying pregnancy weight in my thighs and mid-section, but at 5'7" and 180 pounds, I still looked good. I took great care of my locs, kept my nails and feet done, and stayed cute. We had a home gym because Darius liked to workout, but after a long day of working, tending to the baby and cooking, I didn't have the energy to get on the treadmill or workout.

As the days turned to months and the months turned to years, we became nothing more than estranged roommates who coexisted for the sake of a child and professional appearances. I tolerated the dysfunction and disrespect because I believed if I continued to love him, he would one day get his shit together and reciprocate the love. I was wrong.

I tried everything I could think of to make us work. Hell, I got sage from Hanifa's garden and burned it in every room of the house, attempting to cleanse it of any negative energy. I meditated, fasted, tried CBD oil, and even considered a rebirth (cutting off my locs), but couldn't go through with it.

I didn't want Yasmin seeing me go through what I had been going through and believe that's what love looks like. I wanted to be the strong mother-figure for her that my mother had been for me. She deserved to live in a healthy environment, even if that meant mommy and daddy weren't together.

After seven, unhappy, happy years, I didn't have anything left to give him. What little of me was left, I was determined to give to my baby, so I told Darius I wanted a divorce. That was nine months ago. In reality, we had been over years ago; I just wasn't ready to accept it.

Darius and I agreed to be cordial around Yasmin, and to be amicable with the divorce. The terms were fair: I would buy him out of the house; we'd split our joint-savings account, 401(k), Facebook stock, and all medical and dental expenses for Yasmin; we'd have joint-custody, but Yasmin would live with me and he could get her every other weekend; he would get the black, Mercedes Benz S550, and I would get the white, Range Rover.

The situation was stressing me out so bad I began experiencing migraine headaches on a regular basis. I struggled with depression, which led to drinking more and 'self-medicating' with marijuana, courtesy of my sister, Hanifa.

My sisters, Hanifa and Michaela, stood by my side through it all. They listened to me vent, cried with me, and were supportive even while dealing with the challenges of their own lives. Hanifa had married Jahsani, gave birth to twins, quit her job to take care of them, and then opened her own business, Lotus, a yoni steaming spa; Jahsani opened and operated his own barbershop. Michaela had been through a couple of high-profile relationships, quit her job at a big marketing firm, and started her own consulting business.

My moment of reflection was interrupted by the sound of someone knocking at my door.

"Come in!" I yelled.

Mrs. Nelly entered with several folders in her hand. "I need your signature on a few things." She carefully looked me over and asked, "Are you alright?"

"I'm fine. I was just thinking about something."

"How's my grandbaby doing?" she smiled, picking up the picture of Yasmin on my desk.

"Into everything and bossing people around," I answered.

"She got it honest."

I playfully stuck my tongue out at her and smiled as I returned the folders to her. Mrs. Nelly turned and left the room.

Although the school's educators were passionate about their work, they were also looking forward to summer break. I loved working with the students and helping them develop. What I despised about the job were the politics and lack of resources needed to ensure every child received a quality education. Every year the budget seemed to decrease, but the expectations didn't. The faculty and I worked hard to make learning fun and interesting for the students, even when it meant paying out of our own pockets to do so.

Me and Yasmin got home around 5pm. My first order of business was kicking off my heels and removing my bra so I could slip into something comfortable. I threw on some grey, yoga pants, a tank top, then let my hair down. My locs were down to the middle of my back.

Yasmin followed me around the kitchen like she was my shadow. On the night's menu was baked chicken, broccoli, and mashed potatoes. I poured a glass of wine and got busy.

While standing at the island mashing potatoes and watching Yasmin play with her toys, I couldn't help but think about the void caused by Darius' absence. No longer did the sound of his deep voice and scented presence fill a room, nor was there the sound of Yas' little laugh and feet scurrying across the wood floors as he chased her into the safety of my arms. One would think that after nine months I'd be used to the silence, but I wasn't.

I walked over to the family room and turned on the stereo. I needed to hear Jhene Aiko to change the mood. My favorite song, *Pussy Fairy*, was playing when my cell phone started ringing. It was Michaela. I answered in my usual Detroit vernacular.

"What up, tho?"

"What you doing?"

"Cooking," I replied, opening the oven to check on the chicken.

"Mmmm, what you making?"

"Bangin' baked chicken, broccoli, and real-deal, mashed potatoes."

"That sounds good. I need to get off this computer and make me something to eat. Where's my niecy-poo at?"

"Playing in the family room. What's up with you?"

"You know the grind don't stop. I just got invited to check out an event this Saturday for the blog and wanted to know if you were free to go with me and Hanifa."

I hadn't been out in months. It was Darius' weekend to have Yasmin, and I didn't have any other plans, so I figured I'd hang.

"Yeah, I'll go with y'all," I said. "Where's Cat Eyes?" I asked, referring to Carl, her boyfriend.

"He just left for work," she answered in a disturbed tone.

Confused, I asked, "What's wrong with that?"

"You know we trying to get a house, so he bidded on a better paying post that just happens to be on third shift. Girl, you know I'm sick. I be needing all that dick to put me to sleep at night."

Unfortunately, I couldn't relate to her dilemma. It had been years since I had my world rocked and put to sleep. The only action I was getting these days was playing with myself in the bathtub.

"Aight, girl, I'll let you get back to cooking," she said. "Holla at me later."

"OK. Peace."

Part of me envied the companionship my sisters had in their lives. Hanifa and Jahsani were still going strong, and Michaela and Carl had been together going on three years.

After eating, I cleaned the kitchen, played with Yas for a while, then went upstairs and gave her a bath; I sat her clothes out for the next day and put her to bed. It had been another long day, and now it was time for me to unwind. I lit the candles in my bathroom, drew me a bath, then went and poured another glass of wine.

I stepped into the water, sat down, and relaxed. The hot water felt amazing. I sipped the wine and closed my eyes, allowing the tranquility of the moment to have sway. Moments later, I thought about this morning's dream and Mr. Perfect. I gently began caressing my melon-sized breasts, squeezing them together. I began caressing my nipples, rolling them between my thumbs and forefingers until they were taut and hard.

My clit was now pulsating. I finished the last of my drink and sat the glass down on the floor. Slowly, I began rubbing my clit in small circles, then slipped two fingers inside and stroked in and out. *Ummm*, I moaned.

Masturbation had become my thing. I knew exactly what to do to get myself off in five minutes. I raised my leg out of the water, letting it hang over the side of the tub while envisioning a sexy, big-dick man fucking the shit out of me. As I increased the pace of my fingers, I took my other hand and rubbed my clit. The surfeit sensation intensified. "Uhh... uhh!" I moaned out, enjoying the bliss coming over me as I came. I sat motionless for a few minutes, relishing the quick fix before bathing and going to bed.

Darius' black, Mercedes Benz pulled into the driveway a little after 1 pm. Our exchange was brief and polite. I updated him on Yasmin's last doctor's visit, and that was the extent of our communication. My lawyer hadn't gotten back with me on the status of the divorce, so for all I knew, things were moving along as they should. Funny thing is, every time I saw Darius, the nurturing aspect of me wondered if we'd ever work things out and get back together.

With Yas gone, I could get a few things accomplished before nightfall. I put on my Jill Scott CD, lit an incense, washed a load of clothes, then cleaned the house. Hanifa was going to wash and style my locs, so after I finished cleaning, I ran to the nail salon to get a manicure and pedicure.

The nail salon was crowded when I arrived, but the wait wasn't too bad. I picked out a pretty, marine-blue polish, then sat in the feet soaking chair. The nail tech handed me a bottled water. As my feet soaked in the warm water, I pressed them on the marbles at the bottom and rolled them back and forth, massaging the arch and heel of each foot. It was extremely relaxing.

While the nail tech worked on my feet, I scrolled through my favorite stores' summer catalogs on my phone. I looked up for a brief moment and saw a handsome, brown-skinned guy staring at me; he was getting a manicure. He didn't look familiar, so I averted my eyes. I looked back to my phone and scrolled down to the children's clothes.

Feeling the energy of being watched, I looked up again and saw the same guy staring at me. This time, he flashed a nice smile at me. Sensing he was flirting with me, I smiled back coyishly. The salon door opened and in walked a tall, white woman with blonde hair. She walked over and kissed my admirer, then sat beside him. I shook my head and returned to the online catalog. If it wasn't for buzzard luck, I wouldn't have any at all.

I pulled up at Hanifa's house around 5 pm. Jahlil and Jahlissa were riding their bikes up and down the sidewalk. The front door was open, so I walked in and yelled out for her.

"Nifaaaa!"

"In the kitchen," she responded.

I entered the kitchen and found her washing dishes.

The smell of fried chicken was in the air. “Smells good in here, momma,” I said while taking a seat at the table.

“Are you hungry?”

“Nah. I’ll grab a bite on my way home.”

“Aight, but it’s more than enough for you.” She smiled at the sight of my hands. “Your nails are cute.”

“Thank you. I see Jahlissa’s finally getting the hang of riding her bike.”

“Girl… that’s the first thing out her mouth when we get home. ‘Mom, can I ride my bike?’” she mimicked Jahlissa.

“You sound just like her, too!” I laughed.

Hanifa left out to get me a towel. I pulled the mango lime oil and loc gel out of my Louis Vuitton Neverfull bag and sat them on the table. Hanifa returned with a towel and her ‘medical’ bag, a purple, Crown Royal bag. She pulled out rolling papers, a hand grinder, and a small bag of weed. When she opened the bag, it smelled like a skunk had walked in and sprayed us.

“Damn, girl!” I said, turning my nose up.

She responded in her best Atlanta voice, “Dis dat gas right here, shawty!”

The weed had an exotic aroma and tasted like Bubblicious Bubble Gum. As we passed it back and forth, we talked about the kids, her spa, fashion, relationships, and the social uprising sweeping over the country of yet another unarmed black man being killed by the police.

The door leading to the garage opened and Jahsani walked in.

"What's hattenin, Brooke?" he energetically asked.

"What up, tho?" I replied, high as a kite.

He walked over and wrapped his arms around Hanifa from behind and kissed on her neck in a loving way. "Hey, Queen."

"Hi, baby. Are you ready to eat?"

"I am, but not that food." He grinded on her. "I had a little time before my next appointment and thought I'd pay my beautiful wife a visit." The sexual implications were obvious.

"I was about to wash and twist Brooke's hair."

He looked at each of us and smiled. "I see y'all having a little pow-wow. I'll get out y'all's way and go kick it with my babies." He spanked Hanifa's butt and left back out.

Watching them interact was a beautiful sight for sore eyes and a wounded heart.

"That's what I'm talking 'bout right there, Nifa. Love, affection, companionship – I miss that so much! The way y'all vibe together is beautiful."

"Sis, you know every marriage is hard work. We have our good and bad days, but there ain't nothing in this world I wouldn't do for Jahsani. It's a war going on outside and our brothers and sisters are being slaughtered in the streets in cold blood. Society and the media are working hard to emasculate our strong, black men, but mine is a king, and within the confines of this house he will be treated as such."

"I know that's right, Nifa!" I championed her sentiments.

Hanifa washed my locs, oiled my scalp, then palm-rolled and braided my locs into a bun. Her speed and styling skills had improved greatly from doing Jahsani's locs over the years. After she finished, we hugged, then I headed home so I could get ready.

I walked in the house and went upstairs to get in the shower. I laid three outfits on the bed and stepped back to get a better look at which one accurately described my mood: chill, fierce, or sexy? Chill won out. I put the others in the closet, then put on a sexy, white, lace panty and bra set, a white Dolce and Gabbana wrap-around dress, a pastel-blue, sleeveless blouse, and a cute pair of sandals.

The event was being sponsored by an up-and-coming fashion designer who had recently opened a boutique. I was always down to support black-owned businesses in any way I could, be it purchasing goods or promoting their services.

Atlanta is the Black Hollywood. Everything is a production, from red carpets and valet parking to premiere lights and photo ops. There was no telling who might be at this event. Sure enough, when I pulled up at the club, there was valet parking and a red carpet. The attendant opened my door, handed me a ticket, then I stepped inside.

There was a nice-sized crowd in attendance. Yo Gotti was blasting through the club's speakers. People stood around talking; some laughing, others just watching. Drinks were flowing. I spotted Hanifa by way of her afro; she and Michaela were standing over by the bar that had a fish tank behind it. I headed in their direction.

"Ladies!" I exclaimed.

"Hey, Brooke," they both said.

I looked out at the crowd and commented, "Looks like a lot of folks came out to support."

"Wait til you see some of her collection. It's dope!" Michaela assured. Several pieces from her summer collection would be modeled throughout the evening.

We were about to order drinks until we were interrupted.

"Hold up, ma. How you doing?" asked a handsome, brown-skinned man. He wore black jeans; a black, fitted, Fendi shirt; belt, loafers; and a diamond bezel Rolex on his wrist.

I paused to see if I recognized him. I didn't. "I'm fine. How are you?"

He smiled. "I'm good, but I'd be better if I can get to know you." "Is that right?"

"Look here, whatever it is that your heart desires, I can make it happen for you."

"I doubt it," I said, annoyed by his statement.

"Ma, we can hit any mall or car lot in the country and run up a check; it's nothing!" he confidently boasted.

"Not interested."

"Give me one good reason why not." He seemed shocked.

"I'll give you two. One, I got my own bag. And two, baby, I vibrate on a higher frequency than you're used to, so you might wanna stick with the low vibrating chicks."

Michaela and Hanifa were cracking up laughing when I turned back to face them.

"Y'all just gon' stand there and laugh, tho? I'm glad my woes can provide y'all's amusement."

Hanifa stopped laughing for a second. "No you didn't hit'em with 'I vibrate on a higher frequency than you're used to'. I like that one!" She continued laughing and shaking her head.

We got our drinks and walked off. And to think, the night was just getting started.

Chapter 2

(Hanifa)

It was another gloomy morning. The forecast called for a 70% chance of rain by noon. Everyone in the house was scrambling to get ready. I made breakfast while Jahlissa and Jahlil were brushing their teeth; Jahsani was in the shower. As usual, I was the first one up but the last one to leave the house. Jahsani dropped the kids off at school on his way to the barbershop. Truly, teamwork makes the dream work.

Our ten-year anniversary was quickly approaching. Jahsani and I still hadn't decided if we were going to celebrate it with family and friends or take a romantic getaway.

Like all married couples, we faced a lot of challenges, but we sacrificed and worked hard. After giving birth to the twins, I told Jahsani I wanted to quit my job as a lab technician to stay home and breastfeed. I wanted to make sure my children's emotional, physical, and mental needs were met. With Jahsani being the loving and supportive husband he was, he was okay with it.

Things were tight in the beginning. We only had one income coming into the house, but he held it down. We both possessed entrepreneurial spirits, so after the kids waned off of being breastfed, I got a small business loan and opened Lotus Steaming Spa. Jahsani recently added mobile barbering to his shop's services. This added feature was for elite clientele, like professional athletes and corporate types. With both of our businesses being successful, we were starting to get ahead.

With all that we had going on, our sex life was no longer spontaneous; rather, we did it whenever it was convenient to do so. Jahsani is easy on the eyes. He's a 6'2", chocolate brother with an athletic build. He has long, pretty locs and is unapologetically African! He was everything I wanted in a man. We made a concerted effort to keep things poppin' by having a date night every other Friday. Role playing and fulfilling each other's fantasy were part of date night.

Due to inclement weather, business was slow. While sitting in the waiting area listening to the relaxing sounds of a tropical rain forest playing from the speaker above, I stared out the window, watching rain beads streak down. All of this had me in a daze. My thoughts were on our date tonight.

My fantasy was to meet a stranger at a bar, fall in love, and go home with him. It's cheesy, but I would never do it real life. Jahsani and I agreed that flirting with other people was permissible in order to make it seem real, but under no circumstances were we to exchange numbers or behave inappropriately. Infidelity has never been an issue in our marriage because we love, trust, and respect one another.

While contemplating a character to play, and deciding on what to wear, two women trotted past the window and walked in. I snapped out of my reverie and went behind the counter.

"Good afternoon, ladies. Welcome to Lotus. Do you have an appointment?" I asked, pulling up the appointment page on the computer.

"No," answered the shorter woman.

"No problem. Have either of you steamed with us before?"

"No," the same woman responded. "One of my girlfriends told me about the experience she had here, so we thought we'd give it a try."

"That's great. Let me explain the health benefits of steaming and the procedure," I said handing them our brochure. "Yoni steaming can help relieve infections; restore your pH balance; tighten and strengthen your uterus; increase circulation, which can increase orgasms; aid with fibroids, regulate menstrual cycles, and assist with ovulation. We understand the sensitive nature of the yoni, so we sanitize every throne before and after each use to ensure you queens have a satisfying and safe experience. Now, the steaming throne is a chair with a hole in it. You put blended herbs in a hot pot of water, put the pot in a box under the seat, and sit on it."

"Can I bring my phone with me?" asked the other woman.

"Sure," I answered before explaining what else was available to the women. "We also have stones and crystals you can use for meditation. If you choose, you can read or listen to music while steaming." Extending my arm to the back, I said, "If you're ready, we can head back and I'll show you your rooms."

They signed the login book, then I escorted them to the back.

Tori, my assistant, agreed to close up the spa so I could pick the kids up from school and drop them off at my mother's house before rush hour traffic. Unfortunately, I still managed to get caught in the gridlock on my way home. The forty-five minute delay put a wrinkle in my plans.

As soon as I got home, I jumped in the shower and washed my hair. I got out and put my hair in two braids to the back, then laid my baby-hair edges down. It was still dreary outside, so I decided to keep it simple but cute. I went in the closet and pulled out my black and white, fitted, Adidas dress and matching shell-toe sneakers. I got dressed while smoking a joint, and now Keisha was ready to come to life!

I arrived at the bar an hour late. Happy Hour was in full swing. Megan Tha Stallion's song *Savage* was blasting out the speakers. Heads were swaying to the beat as people stood around talking and enjoying the end of the work week. There was an empty seat at the end of the bar, so I sat in it. I scanned the crowd for signs of Jahsani, but I didn't see him. Minutes later, a female bartender placed a drink in front of me on a napkin.

"Here you go, beautiful. Courtesy of the gentlemen over there," she pointed over to the couch area.

I looked and saw Jahsani sitting in a chair talking with three females. I sipped the drink to see what he ordered. It was Blackberry Ciroc, and it was strong. Right away, I knew he was trying to get me lit. we made eye contact, and I raised my glass to say thanks. He smiled and winked at me. Game on!

Judging from appearances, the four of them were having a good time. Each of the girls had a drink in hand and were laughing at something he said. One of them was sitting on the arm of his chair, playfully stroking his locs. Clearly, she was flirting with him. From what I could see, she was cute with an attractive figure, and possibly in her late 20s or early 30s. Part of me was annoyed that she was fondling my husband's hair, but I stayed in character. Keeping it cool, I sipped my drink and vibed with the music.

A tall light-skinned guy with hazel eyes came up and stood next to me. He ordered a drink and then turned towards me.

"How you doing, gorgeous?"

"I'm good. And yourself?"

"I can't complain. What's your name?"

"Keisha." It felt funny using my alias.

"Tony," he said, shaking my hand. "Why you sittin' alone?"

"Who said I was alone?"

He laughed. "My bad. You got a man?"

"I do."

"Makes sense. You're too beautiful to be single."

"Thank you."

He got his drink and walked off.

I glanced back over to where Jahsani was, but he was no longer there; only the females were. I finished my drink and asked the bartender for a bottle of water. Ashanti's song *Baby* started playing, so I stood up and did my pretty girl two-step while singing the lyrics. Several guys in my area were checking me out, then out of nowhere I was tapped on my shoulder. I turned around and saw Jahsani. He was dressed in blue jeans, a navy-blue Polo shirt, and white Yeezy's. he had a bright smile on his face.

"Pardon self, Queen. How you doing?"

Still jamming to the song, I replied, "I'm good."

"I'm Jason. What's your name, luv?"

"Keisha."

"Where you from, Keisha?"

"The westside," I said, struggling not to laugh.

"Well, Keisha from the westside, you got a man?" He moved closer into my space.

"It's complicated," I flirtatiously stated.

"All situationships are," he joked. "What you drinking?"

"Surprise me."

"Say less."

He ordered us a round of Blackberry Ciroc. We sat at the bar talking, laughing, and flirting with each other as if we were complete strangers. Looking at his dilated pupils, I could tell he'd been smoking and had more than the three drinks we had. This was a wonderful sign because that tipsy dick be the best.

He leaned in and whispered in my ear, "I bet yo' man can't fuck you better than me." The tone of his voice was sexy and sent chills down my spine. I sipped my drink, holding his gaze with temptress eyes.

He caressed my thigh, then leaned in and whispered in my ear again, "I bet yo' man can't eat that pussy better than me." He then sucked on my neck. The moistness of his lips made my pussy so wet I thought I was going to cum that very instance. It was time to go! Once we finished our drinks, I took him by the hand and walked out the bar.

As soon as we walked in the house, we headed upstairs to our bedroom. I lit the candles on the nightstands, then pushed up on him and we started kissing. He rubbed and squeezed my butt while I groped the bulge in his jeans straining at the fabric, begging to be released.

I unfastened his jeans, pulled his hard dick out, then kneeled and put it in my mouth. The wetness of my mouth soaked his dick as I took it in and out, then licked around the head like it was a Charms Blow-pop. "Get it, Keisha," he uttered in approval. Sucking his dick brought me just as much satisfaction as it did him.

After helping him out of his pants, I stopped and took my clothes off. I then laid back on the bed, anxious to receive his good loving. He crawled between my legs until we were face to face. We kissed, smacking as we tasted each other's mouth. He kissed my neck, my breasts, and sucked on both nipples, then he slowly kissed down my body until his face was on top of my pussy.

My body desperately craved his touch. Suddenly, I felt his wet tongue lick up and down my pussy lips, then slide between them and began licking and sucking my clit. "Ooh, baby," I moaned in delight.

He looked up at me and continued to lick with long, deep laps. His strong hands hooked under my legs and pulled me closer until my pussy was pressed against his mouth. He flickered his tongue across my clit. My legs began trembling uncontrollably as my orgasm unfurled. "Ooh, baby, this yo' pussy! This yo' pussy!" I moaned vociferously.

Before I could gather my bearings, I felt the tip of his dick sliding inside of my soaking, wet pussy. The first few strokes were slow and deep, just the way I like it. We had mastered each other's body and love frequencies over the years, so he knew every spot I wanted to be touched, how much pressure to apply, and when to increase the pace. He was holding back, teasing me with short, shallow strokes, so I tossed my legs around his neck and tugged at his waist.

"Gimme that dick," I softly requested.

"You want all this dick, Keisha?" he asked, looking into my eyes.

I needed and wanted him to ram it all in. "I wanna feel all that dick," I fervently moaned.

He picked up the pace and delved deeper inside of me. I moaned louder and louder. "Yes, yes, yes! This yo' pussy! This yo' pussy!" I screamed as the pleasurable sensation of another orgasm washed over me.

Jahsani was thrusting so hard that beads of sweat rolled off of his forehead and onto my breasts. I could tell by his heavy breathing he was on the verge of cummin'. "Aaaah, shit!" he groaned, letting my legs down as he collapsed on top of me. Knowing his dick was extra sensitive after nutting, I rolled him onto his back and commenced to sucking the tip of it. I'd grown fond of the taste of his cum mixed with my juices. He started squirming, trying to get away, but I held him down with my free hand as his legs twitched. I sucked and stroked his shaft until he went totally limp. He was comatose.

I snuggled up on his chest and we drifted off to sleep.

Chapter 3

(Michaela)

My Wednesday morning was a productive one. I went to the gym, stopped at the dealership and got an oil change, picked up a few items from the grocery store, and took a refreshing shower. I still had a couple of hours before it was time for my 2pm hair appointment with my hairdresser and homegirl Carmen, so I slipped on some blue-lace boy-shorts, went into the living room, and opened my HP laptop computer.

One of the luxuries of working at home for myself was that I clocked in whenever I felt like it. A second luxury was that there was no dress code. I seldom wore clothes in the house, or to bed for that matter. You could say I'm a bit of a purist who is most comfortable in my own skin. Whenever I did put on something, it was either one of Carl's t-shirts, a tank-top, or some panties.

Carl and I met three years ago at the gym. I was on the elliptical machine when a 6'4", light-skinned, well-built guy with green eyes got on the one next to me. Unlike many of the other thirst-buckets who came on to me at the gym, he didn't simply just gawk and drool over my body. We chatted, and after the workout he asked me to join him at the juice bar down the street.

Our relationship grew after that day. Lately, we've been discussing taking things to the next level: living together and having children. I had put off having kids after walking way from my job in corporate America in order to pursue my own consulting business. But I'm not getting any younger and would one day love to have a family of my own.

Carl is 41 years of age and already has a 12-year-old son from a previous relationship. He's been a supervisor at the Postal Service for 16 years. Because we both have a lot of stuff, we agreed it would be easier to buy a house together rather than cram into my condo or his townhome.

I can honestly say I'm in love with Carl. He has a good heart, great personality, and by far the biggest package I've ever encountered. When hard, its length and girth resemble a fivemonth old baby's leg, and his balls are the size of duck eggs. And the best part is that he's a stone-cold freak who loves to lay in bed all day, exploring and taking my body to higher heights of pleasure.

He stays at my place three nights a week; well, he used to. Carl recently took a third-shift post that came with unlimited overtime. The change in his shift abruptly disrupted our sex lives and, honestly, I'm not too happy about it. But he's doing it for a good reason. The extra money is going towards the down payment on our house, a house big enough to fit both of our needs; a house we could grow into. I've spent a lot of time with Carl's son and have gotten attached to him. We both look forward to his visits, so he will have his own room.

I opened my first email. It was a request from a woman seeking to get a cosmetic line in U.S. stores. After reading her email, I responded by requesting a dossier on her company and a time we could have a Zoom meeting. I sent her a contract with my fees in case she wanted to move forward.

It was opportunities like this that made me walk away from being a chief brand officer for five years. The lack of inclusion and representation of black-owned brands gave me the idea to set up my own consulting business to help people in ways that would have long-term impacts. My consulting business led to me starting a blog as a side hustle. It promotes businesses and events throughout the Atlanta metropolitan area, and I also use it to promote my business to potential clients.

After posting and responding to questions on my blog page, I went in my room to get dressed. I put on some fashion leggings, a crop denim top, my Louie Vuitton denim sneakers and crossbody, then hopped in my Porsche truck and left.

Carmen is my day one. We grew up together in Bowen Homes projects and danced on the high school dance team. She's ATL to the fullest. She was sitting in her chair waiting on me when I walked into the salon.

"What it do, shawty?" I greeted her.

"Hey, girl. You look cute. I like them sneaks and crossbody." She got up so I could sit down.

"Thanks. What's going on with you?"

"Same ol' stuff... stacking this coin, the kids, and Will's simple ass," she joked. "What up with you?"

"You already kno', the grind don't stop. Me and Carl been looking for a house, and that's about it."

She put the apron around my neck. "I saw that event you posted about the other day. It was lit!"

"Yeah. She's a dope designer. Check her out sometime."

Being in Carmen's chair always took me back to the days she did my hair in her mother's kitchen. We'd talk about how our families were doing, her kids, their fathers, people we grew up with, and what the buzz in the city was. She had all the tea.

Today's gossip was about some off-the-chain chat she's a part of. It discusses all the latest freaky things to try with your man to improve your sex life. Of all things, that was one area I didn't have to worry about because my pussy is Aquafina, and I handles my business and bussit wide open for my baby. Nevertheless, I saved the site in my phone just to see what young tenders were out there doing in those streets.

Carmen laid my hair out in a cute pixie cut, as always. Satisfied, I paid and tipped her $20.

"See you next week," I said, heading for the door.

"Aight. Be safe."

I thought about Carl during the ride home. It had been a week since I felt his body against mine, so I was fiending for him. I started dialing his number but stopped after realizing he'd be up in a couple of hours. I didn't want to wake him. The new shift completely rearranged his sleeping schedule, and he was just getting used to it. Being the considerate person I am, I left a message on his voicemail.

I checked my emails upon entering the house and saw that Lauren had signed the contract and sent over the information I requested. I grabbed a smoothie out of the refrigerator, then sat down to go to work.

Lauren's dilemma wasn't uncommon; in fact, I was consulted on a similar situation prior to Lauren, so I knew the scope of work I'd be doing. The quickest and easiest approach was to create a three-tiered outline. First, I'd research the national statistics, industry market share, and merchandising data.

The things I found out were not an anomaly of corporate America, especially when it came to dealing with AfricanAmerican brands. Most large cosmetic retailers rarely, if ever, carried products from black-owned brands. Only 3% did.

Although African-Americans are some of the biggest beauty product consumers, mainstream outlets have consistently ignored our beauty brands. Last year alone, black shoppers spent $473 million on haircare. Haircare itself is a $4.2 billion industry. So, while small, black businesses are dying, white stores and brands are profiting off of black dollars.

Brand recognition is the biggest hurdle most entrepreneurs like Lauren faced. It is very difficult for black-owned and black-funded brands to grow without it. And then there's the lack of connections and capital needed to get the business off the ground.

After spending four hours researching, reading data, and jotting down potential solutions that would help Lauren's business achieve its goals, I closed my laptop and made something to eat. It was getting late, and Carl was heavily on my mind. This was usually the time we'd be lying in bed talking, laughing, watching TV, or making love.

Hoping to ease my mind and body of the tension his absence caused, I poured a glass of wine and took a long, hot bath. When I got out the tub, I laid on my bed to air dry. My moment of solace was interrupted when my phone started ringing. It was Carl; he was Facetiming me. I answered the phone, excited to see his face. "Hey, baby."

"What's going on, beautiful?"

"Nothing much. Just got out the tub, wishing you was here," I said, giving him a solicitous stare.

"Mmmm... so do I. You laying there with all that candy on display; let me see som'em!" he said, grinning like a cheshire cat.

Virtual fourplay was part of our repertoire, and tonight I was all game. "What you wanna see in the candy shop, baby?" I asked seductively.

"Let me see them chocolate gum drops."

I lowered the phone so he could see my titties. I caressed and pinched my nipples. "I wish it was your lips and tongue on them," I said in a dulcet voice.

He licked his lips and smiled. "Let me see that juicy waterfall," he requested.

I spread my legs and held the phone in front of my waxed pussy. Using my free hand, I rubbed my clit in small circles, parted my lips, then slipped a finger inside and licked it dry. "Mmmm... I wish you were here sucking on this pussy right now," I teased.

"Tru that, baby! I wanna taste all that." The salacious look in his eyes and facial expressions were making me hornier. "Do that one thang, baby." The smile on his face was as big as the state of Texas.

I had learned a few things from my days of dancing and core training. If I contracted my vaginal muscles, my lips would twitch as if they were winking. This simple trick could milk a dick as if my lips were giving a hand-job. I zoomed in so he had a close-up view, then I performed my magic.

"Ooooo-weeee! Damn, you som'em special, Michaela!"

His reaction fueled my burning desire, so I placed a pillow in front of my pussy to prop the phone up and free my other hand.

"I miss you kissing me here," I said, spreading my lips and rubbing my clit. "I miss you licking me here." I rubbed up and down, side to side. "And I miss you putting that big dick deep inside here." I inserted two fingers inside my pussy and slowly stroked in and out. "Ssss, aaaah!" I sighed in delight.

"Damn, baby, you got my dick over here rock hard!"

"Good. Pull it out so I can see it," I commanded in a sultry tone while fingering myself. He pulled his dick out. There it was in all its glory – big, long, and strong. "Stroke it for me, daddy." Slowly, Carl began stroking it. "I wish I could put all that dick in my mouth right now and suck every drop out of it, daddy."

"I love how you suck this dick, baby. You're not afraid of it, and you don't try to be all neat. You slob all over it, slurp on it, and deep throat it like it's special to you," he said, steady stroking his dick.

The tone of his voice and the thought of all that meat inside me had me about to explode, so I began fingering myself faster. The sloshing sound from my wetness sounded like splashing water. "Ooo, daddy. I'm 'bout to cum."

He stroked his dick faster.

As the sensation surged through my body, my back arched off the bed. "Oooo… oooo… ehhh!" I screamed and shuddered in ecstasy as my orgasm unfurled.

"I'm cummin', too, baby!" he groaned then exploded on a towel.

I laid motionless with my eyes closed, tickled by what just went down. "See how you got me over here fiendin' for you," I said, showing him the puddle in the sheets.

"The feeling is mutual, baby."

Enticingly, I said, "I need to see you tomorrow."

"Aight. Let me get myself together before someone come in here."

"Have a safe shift. Love you."

"Love you, too, baby."

After I cleaned myself up, I changed the bedding and went to sleep.

The next morning, I went to the gym, then came home and got straight to work on tier two for the client. Tier two dealt with cost of customer acquisition and production cost vs retail. Once I saw what it cost to market the products to her targeted demographic, combined with the cost of a single unit, I was able to determine the price point that would appeal to customers and be profitable to her bottom line.

I took a break around noon. I needed to run a few errands, so I took a shower and got dressed. I threw on some holey jeans, a tank-top, my Tony Burch sandals and crossbody, and was out the door.

The nail salon was around the corner from my condo, so I stopped there first to get a manicure and pedicure. I left there and went to the bank to speak with a loan officer about financing for a house. He checked our credit scores and informed me that we were pre-approved for a $400,000 loan. Excited, I called Carl as soon as I exited the bank. His phone went straight to voicemail. More than likely, I figured, he was asleep, so I left him a message to call me.

On my way back home, I stopped at the Cellar and bought a couple bottles of wine to celebrate. Being pre-approved for such an amount meant we could find the home we really wanted. When I got home, I called a few realtors. In fact, I dedicated the rest of the day to looking for houses online. I wanted to see what was on the market within our price range.

I called it quits around 9:30pm. I warmed up the leftover seafood pasta I made two days ago. While eating, it dawned on me that Carl didn't come by or return my call from earlier. He was at work by now. I poured a glass of wine. After a few sips, the Bowen Homes in me kicked in. I decided I was going to pull up on him.

I went in the bedroom and opened the dresser with all my sexy lingerie in it. I selected a set, then jumped in the shower. I washed, got out, and went back to my room to get dressed. Still sipping on the glass of wine, I rubbed Jimmy Choo body lotion over my body. I put on my sexy, red, laced panties and stockings. I clasped the garter belt and put my bra on. The red, Christian Louboutin heels were next. Although they're stylish, they're extremely uncomfortable. Luckily, this mission didn't call for me to be on my feet at all. I sprayed on a light mist of Jimmy Choo perfume, then put on a tan tunic and headed out.

Butterflies swirled in my stomach as I got closer to his job. I turned onto the grounds of the Postal Service and headed for the loading docks. Carl's white Escalade was backed up against the building. I parked next to it, then called his phone. He answered on the second ring.

"Hello?"

"Hey, baby. Are you busy?"

"Not at the moment. The next truck ain't due for another thirty minutes. How's your day been?"

"Busy! I've got a new client, so I've been working on that," I said. "What happened to you today?"

"My bad, baby. I was beat when I got off. I went home and crashed."

"Oh, guess what happened today," I excitedly quipped.

"What?"

"I stopped by the bank earlier to talk to a loan officer, and we have been pre-approved for $400,000!"

Surprised, he exclaimed, "That's great, baby!"

"I know, right?"

"You been on my mind heavy since last night."

"Yeah, yeah... you don't miss me," I said playfully.

"Shittin' me. More than you know, baby."

"Well, step outside for a minute and let me lay my eyes on you."

"You here?" he asked surprised.

"Parked next to your truck."

"Here I come."

Seconds later, the door swung open and Carl emerged from the building. He opened the passenger door and the interior light came on. I was in the back with my right leg on the backrest, and my left leg cocked on the middle console. His eyes lit up like lights on a Christmas tree when he saw me with the tunic wide open.

"Clawd, have mercy!" he said, biting his knuckles. He jumped in the back and shut the door.

Conscious of the limited time we had, I straddled his lap and kissed him. "See how much I miss you," I whispered in his ear, then nibbled on his neck.

Rubbing my butt, he replied, "I do, baby."

"I know you been working 16-hour days so we can get the house we want, so I wanted to come show you how much I appreciate and miss you, baby."

I passionately kissed him. The passion and lust infused the intertwining of our tongues, which made my nipples stiffen and my pussy tingle. By the bulging mound beneath me, I could tell he was aroused, too. I unfastened his belt and pants while he sucked on my neck.

"Damn, Michaela," he heavily panted. "You smell amazing, baby."

Growing impatient from anticipation, Carl pulled the crotch of my panties to the side and guided his massive dick inside of me. "Aaaahh!" I gasped in delight of the instant surge of pleasure. "Yes! That's what I'm talkin' 'bout right there, baby!"

Feeling him inside of me was the equivalent of an addict getting a fix. With each stroke, my pussy got wetter and wetter. His big hands squeezed my voluptuous cheeks, pulling them apart so he could thrust deeper into me. The scent and sounds of sex quickly filled the vehicle.

"Michaela Jackson, it is not humanly possible for anyone's pussy to get this wet, baby!" he said, enthralled by the sloshing sound of him gliding in and out.

His compliment gassed me up, so I rocked back and forth even faster, poppin' it on his dick, making the sound even louder.

"Ride that dick, baby!"

Now feeling myself, I transitioned from my knees to squatting on my feet. I began bouncing up and down real fast and hard, making my ass smack against his thighs. "Like that, daddy?" I asked, moaning at a feverish pitch.

The intense sensation of his dick constantly massaging my clit had me about to explode. "Yes... yes... yessss!" I screamed as I orgasmed and came to a halt.

Carl continued stroking like he was in the gym doing pelvic thrusts with weight across his waist. This was one of the reasons I was so in love with him. He wasn't timid or intimidated by all this ass; he knew just how to handle it. His pace and groans increased, so I knew he wouldn't last much longer. "Auhhh," he groaned, burying his dick deep up inside of me while squeezing my butt as he erupted.

As the electrifying sensation rendered us lying motionless in a warm embrace, I decided to use my magic. I contracted my pussy muscles and milked his dick until our epic sexcapade was interrupted by a voice on his walkie-talkie.

"Big C, the truck just pulled in. You want me to start processing it?"

"Hold on," responded Carl, "I'll be right there."

He kissed me and gave my butt a love tap. "That was great, baby. Let me get back in here before they fuck something up."

I slowly dismounted so he could pull up his pants. My panties were soaking wet. "Stop by when you get off and I'll have breakfast ready for you," I enticingly stated.

"Aight. Drive safely, baby." He kissed my forehead before exiting the vehicle.

I tied my tunic, then got out and saw how wet the seat was. I knew my first stop after leaving the gym would be to get my truck detailed. What can I say? Sometimes a sister's got to do what a sister's got to do.

Chapter 4

(Brooke)

School was out. Except for a couple of teachers packing up their classrooms, the building was empty. I loaded the last box into my truck and happily headed home to start summer break. I had three goals for the summer: go to the gym in the morning time with Michaela, work with Yasmin on cognitive and speaking skills, and restore my mind and spirit to harmonic balance.

Michaela had always worked out to keep her body tight and fit. I knew she would push me in a positive way. Our first day of working out was physically taxing, but I was determined to push through and stick with it. By the second week, my endurance had improved, and my body didn't ache as much the day after. Our morning workouts were a double blessing. They allowed us to catch up on girl-talk while burning calories at the same time.

I worked with Yasmin on identifying and saying the primary colors. She could recognize and say 'red' and 'blue' blocks with ease, but like most kids she struggled with yellow and green, saying them in the cutest way – 'lellow' and 'gween'. Her smile, innocent eyes, and warm hugs were therapeutic for me because of my relationship woes. I spent many days and sleepless nights questioning whether or not I was to blame for Darius no longer loving me. Could I have been a better wife? Even after all this time, part of me wondered if we should try again for Yasmin's sake.

Thursday evening, Yasmin and I were snuggled up on the couch reading her favorite book, *Cat in the Hat* by Dr. Seuse, when my cell phone started ringing. I picked it up and saw it was Michaela.

"Hello?"

"Hi, momma. What you up to?"

"Reading *Cat in the Hat* for the thousandth time," I said jokingly.

"You know that's niecy-poo's favorite book," she laughed. "Anyway, one of Jahsani's clients owns Cultural Expressions Art Gallery in Mid-Town and is having a showing Saturday at 7pm. I thought you might like to come check it out."

"I've never heard of the place."

"Neither had I, but it's an upscale event, so it should be nice. Plus, you can wear something sexy to show off all the hard work you been putting in at the gym, Ms. Thang!" she said in a sassy tone.

I hadn't been out since the last time I met Michaela and Hanifa at the club and was approached by that bozo. It was time to step out again.

"Sure. I'll go. Is Hanifa going?"

"You already know Poetic Justice going," she said facetiously.

"You silly. Aight. Let me go because my boss is getting impatient and roughly turning the pages."

"Later, chic."

"Peace."

Despite our separation, Darius's mother and I were on good terms. She called to check up on Yasmin on a regular basis. Needing a babysitter for later on, I called and asked if she'd watch Yasmin while I attended the showing at the art gallery. Having been a single mother herself, Ms. Patterson knew the daily challenges and emotional toll mothering had on me, so she was always willing to keep her granddaughter so I could have a moment to myself.

Darius's black Mercedes Benz was in her driveway when I pulled up to her house. I let Yasmin out of the car seat, grabbed her bag, then walked to the door. Darius opened it as I was about to knock. He had an eerie look on his face, but I wasn't about to let him ruin my day. I spoke and walked right past him into the living room where his mother was sitting on the sofa.

"There goes Nanna's grandbaby!" exclaimed an excited Ms. Patterson. "Come gimme a hug!" Yasmin giggled and left her father as she sped to her nanna. Ms. Patterson's open arms wrapped her in a tight squeeze.

Sitting Yasmin's bag in a chair, I prepared to leave. "Ms. Patterson, I'll call you as soon as it's over to let you know I'm on my way."

"Don't worry about us. Enjoy yourself; we'll be here when you get back." Turning to Yasmin, she said, "Ain't that right, Yas?" Her tickles made Yasmin giggle and fold up.

Darius couldn't wait to say something. "Where you going?"

I started to yell 'I'm grown' but decided to be civil. "I'm going to an art showing if you must know." I spoke as calmly as I could.

"What? You dating?"

That inquiry, I ignored. I kissed Yasmin, then left.

It was a gorgeous, sunny afternoon, so I opened the sunroof to enjoy the breeze. While rolling down the expressway, my thoughts fluctuated between what to wear and what Darius's motive was for asking if I was dating. Was he jealous? Did it upset him that someone else wanted me? Or was he having second thoughts about the divorce?

As soon as I got home, I headed up to my bedroom and went in the closet to find something nice to put on. My eyes gravitated to the black, off the shoulder dress I wore to the Maxwell concert last year. I pulled it out and stood in front of the mirror with it up against my body to see how I felt about it. It was tasteful and accentuated my curves. I paired it with a sexy pair of stiletto sandals and then went to take a shower.

Finding a close parking spot was more challenging than I anticipated. Parking was so bad that I didn't get inside the gallery until 7:20pm. The event was extravagant and buzzed with well-dressed people who were socializing, checking out sculptures, artifacts, paintings, and photos. A server stopped in front of me and offered a glass of champagne, which I accepted.

This showing prompted Atlanta's black elite to come out and support. I took a sip of champagne and scanned the room. I recognized several professors of black academia from surrounding colleges, journalists from the Atlanta Tribune, and a few political figures.

While strolling through the gallery looking for signs of either Michaela or Hanifa, I came upon the display of a beautiful 9" African mask. The broad nose and full lips were expressly carved with great artistry. Out of nowhere, a handsome, chocolate brother in a tailored, black suit pulled up beside me. He had long locs that were neatly tied in a fishtail fashion.

"It's a 17th century, ivory mask from the Bibi tribe in ancient Benin, known today as Nigeria. It was worn on the ceremonial belt of a great chief. It represents royal power, intelligence, and authority."

His knowledge of the mask was impressive.

"Forgive me, queen. I'm Seven," he introduced himself with an extended hand.

"Brooke," I replied, shaking his hand.

"I noticed you checking out the mask and couldn't resist coming over to say something to you."

"Well, I'm glad you did."

"Enjoy the rest of your evening, Brooke." He flashed a sexy smile before walking off.

There was something uniquely special about him. Not only was he handsome and educated, but his aura and energy were beautiful. His eyes were warm and inviting, and he had a regal strut.

Minutes later, I spotted Michaela and Carl looking at an abstract painting. Hanifa and Jahsani were standing only a few feet behind them. Michaela wore a sexy, black, bodycon dress with cute sandals. The fellas looked sharp, but Hanifa was giving it to the people in that purple jumpsuit and sandals; her hair was in two afro puffs.

"Hi, fellas," I said, greeting them with hugs. "What's up, ladies?" I hugged the girls.

"You look nice," said Michaela.

"Thanks, boo. I see Nifa channeling her inner Foxy Brown, looking like Cleopatra Jones... you a bad maáma jamma!" I joked.

"Watcho mouth," Hanifa shot back, mimicking the '70s icon of black cinema.

I had to give my girl her props. "I love them afro puffs, Nifa!"

"Thanks. You just getting here?"

"Nah. I was checking out a few things while looking for y'all." Looking around, I added, "This is really nice."

"It is nice," seconded Michaela.

We were looking at a painting when, suddenly, the loud sound of African drumming began. Everyone's attention turned in the direction of a small platform stage where three, shirtless, black men with their faces painted in tribal art beat on a drum and jimbe like they were signaling or communicating something. Six women in ceremonial outfits stood by.

The crowd drew closer to the stage as the deep rhythm ramped up. People pulled out phones and began recording. The break in the drumming cued the women, who started walking in a circle. As the beat ramped back up, they started dancing, twirling, jumping, and gyrating like a spirit had mounted their bodies. Michaela was all into it. She loved all forms of choreographed dancing.

Minutes later, the intense drumming abruptly stopped, and so did the dancers. The gallery erupted in applause, whistles, and camera flashes. The performers bowed. And then the handsome brother who told me about the mask took to the stage.

"Give it up one more time for Atlanta's own African Arts Dance Ensemble." He clapped his hands as everyone gave the performers another round. "It is an African tradition to commemorate those from our community for their accomplishments, as well as life works with song and dance.

"What they just performed was a ritual invoking the presence of our ancestors and the forces of nature to commune with us in celebrating these amazing artists whose creations are present today.

"We're thankful for everyone coming out to support. There are several works for sale, so don't be shy. If we don't support our art, who will? Enjoy the rest of the evening."

He exited the stage. His speech was moving and well received by those in attendance. I watched him mingle with the crowd from the corner of my eye. It was sexy.

He noticed me staring at him. I was too intrigued and entranced to look away. He shook hands with the man and woman he was talking to, then walked in our direction. Our eyes were locked on one another's. And then he and Jahsani embraced in a brotherly hug.

"Peace, king. Glad y'all could make it," said Seven.

"Peace. Seven, this is my queen, Hanifa." Eyeing Hanifa, Jahsani continued, "Baby, this is Seven. He owns the gallery."

Seven shook Hanifa's hand. "It's a pleasure to meet you, queen."

"Likewise, king. This is a beautiful gallery you have, and the artists are dope."

"Thank you."

Jahsani then introduced the rest of us to Seven. "These are our friends. This is Michaela and her boyfriend, Carl."

"Peace, king. Peace, queen," said Seven, shaking their hands.

"And this is Brooke."

"We've met already," said Seven, smiling at me.

Instantly, I felt a stirring between my thighs. I took a sip of my drink, hoping to cool down.

"So, Brooke, has anything else caught your eye tonight?" asked Seven.

I wasn't sure if he was talking about art or me staring at him, so I threw something out. "There's a painting over there of Siamese women connected at the shoulders being dressed by an elder woman. Can you tell me a little about it?"

"Sure. The painting is by a talented brother from Cincinnati named Gilbert Young. He has a lot of great paintings and portraits," he stated. "You have a great eye for art."

Blushing, I replied, "I don't know 'bout all that, but it's a beautiful piece."

He pointed at a chair on display made of Battic birch wood; it had two cylinders for the backrest. "Take this piece for example. Nature has a way of producing the most beautiful patterns, colors, and textures."

The way he looked at me while speaking gave me the impression he used the chair as an analogy for me. Seven then asked two questions that almost left me speechless.

I hope I'm not stepping on any toes, but would it be possible to get your number and call you some time? Maybe take you to lunch or dinner?"

Michaela was standing just outside of his peripheral. She silently encouraged me with animated facial expressions to say yes.

"Sure," I answered, putting my number in his phone.

I watched him walk away and then turned to my girls. They were nodding their heads in approval of me giving Seven my number.

Me and the girls spent the remainder of the evening making our way around the gallery, taking in the works of art and sculptures. After seeing everything on display, we left.

As soon as I got in my truck, I called Ms. Patterson to let her know I was on my way. She, however, insisted I enjoy a night to myself and pick Yasmin up the next morning. She didn't have to tell me twice. I hadn't had a good night's rest in a while, so a night alone was fine by me. I looked forward to sleeping in.

Because my body was still used to waking up at 5:30am, sleeping in was impossible. I laid restlessly in my bed for as long as I could. By 7, I was up. I put on my robe and headed downstairs. I went into the kitchen and turned on the expresso machine.

The early morning sounds of nature were on display outside, so I opened the back door and stepped onto the back porch to listen more closely and enjoy the fresh air. There was something peaceful about witnessing the majesty of nature in the morning. Birds chirping. Insects buzzing. Blades of grass crackling from receiving the sun's life-force. I even heard the sound of a woodpecker pecking a tree off in the distance.

I held onto a cup of coffee as I sat in a deck chair. While peering out into the yard, thoughts of Seven entered my mind. I couldn't quite put my finger on what it was about him that made me feel and react the way I had around him. I mean, the mere presence of the man caused a biological reaction in me. He gave me butterflies like I was a teenage girl infatuated with an older boy. But above all that were his eyes – the way he looked at me.

Since Yasmin would be out of my way for a few more hours, I put on Earth, Wind, and Fire's soulful song, *Devotion*, and started cleaning the lower level of my house. I washed a couple of loads of clothes, folded, and put them away.

By noon, the fresh scents of Pine Sol and Black Love incense permeated the house. I had just got out the tub when my phone started ringing in the bedroom. I didn't recognize the number when I picked it up.

"Hello?"

"Good afternoon, beautiful."

My heart fluttered. It was Seven.

"Good afternoon."

"Did I catch you at a good time?"

"You did."

"I know I'm breaking protocol, but you've been on my mind all night. Hope you don't mind me calling so soon."

"Not at all. You've been on my mind as well," I admitted, sitting on the edge of the bed.

"Good. Are you free for brunch?"

Emotionally, I wasn't sure if I was ready to start seeing anyone, but the idea of brunch seemed harmless... plus I was hungry.

"Sure," I answered.

"Are you familiar with Jackie's Breakfast Nook?"

"I love Jackie's."

"Aight. How long you need?"

"I can be there in forty-five minutes."

"I'll see you then, beautiful."

"Peace."

I moisturized my body with whipped, African shea butter before getting dressed. I put on some red shorts and a white tshirt with a heart on it that read 'I love teaching'. Next, I put on my red and white Nike Air Max '97s and headed out to meet Seven.

Seven was standing outside of Jackie's when I pulled up and parked across the street. He was wearing blue jean shorts, a white, short-sleeve button-up, and a fresh pair of Nike Air Force 1s. The smile on his face grew larger as I crossed the street.

"Glad you could make it, gorgeous."

"Thanks for the invite," I replied as he held the door for me.

He asked the waitress if we could sit in the empty booth by the front window. She seated us there and handed us two menus.

"Can I get you anything to drink?" she asked.

Like a gentleman, Seven allowed me to go first. "I'll have a glass of water with lemons."

"And I'll have a glass of pineapple juice, please."

"I'll get those right out to you," said the waitress before walking off.

I picked up the menu and began looking for what I wanted. Seven initiated the conversation.

"Did you enjoy yourself last night?"

"I did. The atmosphere was chill, and I saw several nice paintings. How long has the gallery been there?"

"Three years now."

The waitress returned with our drinks. "Are you ready to order, or do you need a minute?" she asked.

"I'll have the shrimp and grits," I said.

"And I'll have the veggie omelet with home fries."

The waitress wrote our orders down, collected the menus, then left.

Seven took a sip of his juice while I squeezed the lemon wedge into my water.

"I need to get something off my chest," he sincerely said, looking longingly into my spirit. "Ever since I laid eyes on you, I haven't been able to get you off my mind. Your energy is so magnetic I had to call you right away."

Flattered, I blushed as butterflies began churning in my stomach.

"So, Brooke... tell me something about yourself."

"What would you like to know?" I countered.

"Whatever you're comfortable with me knowing."

"My name is Brooke Patter, sorry, Collins," I corrected myself. "I have a beautiful three-year-old daughter named Yasmin... and I'm the principal at Frederick Douglas Elementary School." I sipped my water.

"Collins? Is that your maiden name?"

"Yes."

"How long were you married?"

"Too long!" I answered, displeased. "Five years."

"It can't be that bad," he chuckled at my demeanor.

"You have no idea," I replied. I sipped my water once more. The mere thought of my marriage began to change my energy, so I took the focus off of me by asking him a question. "How does a handsome brother such as yourself come to own a gallery?"

He leaned back and spoke seriously. "At an early age, my grandfather taught me how to appreciate the beauty of nature, the things people created or painted. After high school, I attended the Art Institute of Chicago, where I earned a degree in architectural engineering. I worked at an engineering firm for a few years, designing shopping malls and residential communities. I learned to invest in commercial real estate with a group of friends, so I walked away from the job to pursue something I was passionate about – art.

"Whenever I went to art shows, seldom did I see any works by black artists or, for that matter, our style of art, so I decided to open a gallery and give black artists a platform to showcase their art to the masses."

His response was different than I expected, but I'm sure it felt good to provide that outlet for others. Well, onto the next question. "How 'bout kids and relationships?" I asked.

"I ended a three-year relationship when I left Chicago, and I don't have any children. I love kids and look forward to having a family in the near future."

The waitress returned and sat our plates on the table, then left. The food looked and smelled delicious. His omelet looked so good it made me second guess my order.

"Can I try some of your omelet?" I asked.

"Help yourself," he said, spinning his plate toward me.

I cut off a chunk and ate it. "Mmm, that's good!"

My mind went from the food back to Seven. The fact he ended his relationship stoked my curiosity. I wondered if his male perspective could shine light on what led to mine and Darius's disconnect.

"If you don't mind me asking, why did you end your relationship?" I ate a spoonful of grits and shrimp.

He dabbed his mouth with a napkin, then took a swig of his juice. "It's hard being in a relationship with a woman who's been dragged through the mud from prior relationships, and she still holds onto the trauma and toxic behaviors from those relationships. It didn't allow her to be emotionally available or open to receive the love I had to give her. I realized the relationship wasn't going anywhere, so I ended it."

There was a brief pause in the conversation as we enjoyed our food. The silence was broken by the sound of his voice. "So, what about your divorce?"

I took a deep breath to gather my thoughts. "To be honest, I'm not sure what caused the initial rift. What I'm sure of is that I loved, respected, and put up with his mood swings, disrespect, and cold attitude until I could no longer do it. I'm not saying I'm perfect, not by a long shot, but I was honest, faithful, and tried to make us work. We've been separated for ten months, but in all actuality it's really been the past four years." I dropped my head and played with my food.

"Pick your head up, queen," he demanded.

I looked up and we locked eyes.

"If you've done your best, you don't have a reason to hang your head. I understand it hurts, but life is cyclical; nothing remains the same, not even love. People outgrow each other, outgrow relationships. You think you failed at marriage?" he asked.

"Obviously... we're getting divorced," I said sarcastically.

"You didn't fail at marriage, Brooke. You learned through experience what a marriage isn't! The only failure in life is not trying," he passionately stated. "Do you know what I see when I look in your eyes?"

I was dying to know the answer. "What?"

"I see the hurt that lies beneath them... but I also see the beauty and grace of your essential-self."

What he said awoke something in my spirit. "What do you mean by that?" I asked, eager to understand.

"The eyes are windows to the soul. They tell a story. By looking into your eyes, I can tell you're a loving, strong woman who's in tune with her higher-self. And, as beautiful as you are, queen, it's not just your adornments that drew me to you." He paused. "I'm drawn to you spiritually because I recognize the divine feminine aspect of the creator in you that is complementary of my divine energy."

Everything in my being started tingling. No man had ever expressed such profound sentiments toward me. Seven was different. His vibe was different. His intellect was different.

"Let me ask you something, Brooke... where are you at this moment in your life? Are you ready to move forward or stay trapped in the past?"

His questions caught me off guard and left me speechless. "Honestly, Seven... I don't know," I admitted with much disheartening. "Can I get back to you on that?"

"Respect. Tell you what, I gotta go to New York for a couple of days, so how 'bout you think about it, and when I get back you let me cook dinner for you and we talk about it then," he suggested.

"Oh, you can cook?" I asked, making a doubtful facial expression.

"I do a little som'em som'em," he smiled.

Handsome, educated, spiritual, and can cook... this acquaintance is shaping up to be too good to be true. I was curious to learn more about him, so I agreed.

Seven paid for brunch, then walked me across the street to my truck, opened the door for me. "Be safe," he said.

"I will. Enjoy the rest of your day." I pulled off to go pick up Yasmin.

Chapter 5

(Brooke)

It had been a month since I started working out with Michaela, and I was beginning to see results. I had more energy, lost 14 pounds, and felt better overall.

We were doing a ten-minute cool down on the treadmill at the end of a workout. Michaela was rambling on about a house she and Carl viewed a few days before, but I wasn't really paying attention. My mind was on the conversation I had with Seven over brunch.

How could a man like him be single in Atlanta, home to so many beautiful women with big butts, degrees from HBCUs, and affiliates of Fortune 500 companies? I mean, he was good looking, humble, educated, and successful. I didn't sense he was gay or a ladies' man. Maybe he wasn't well-endowed, I speculated, trying to make sense of the matter.

Something inside of me clicked while driving home. I was tired of running from the inevitable, and decided it was time to have a one-on-one with myself – the good, the bad, and the ugly. I walked in the house and headed upstairs to run a hot bath. I added a few drops of rose oil into it, then lit the lavender candle on the counter. I pinned my locs up, then took my clothes off and got in the tub.

The water was perfect. I sank until the water crested just below my chin. It wasn't long before the conversation with Seven began replaying in my mind as if it was on a loop – am I ready to move forward or remain trapped in the past?

I knew filing for divorce was just a legal formality, albeit the first step, but moving forward meant much more. *Am I truly ready to let go of Darius?* The answer to that question was *no*. But why? For years I'd held onto hope that we would work it out, fall back in love with one another, and make our family whole again. As I thought about the past, I realized the nostalgia of how things were when we first met was what I had been clinging onto.

Tears began to well in my eyes. It was apparent that we had outgrown one another and our relationship. The notion that I had failed was absurd. Our marriage just wasn't the lifetime union I originally longed for. The tears trickled from my eyes as I realized a chapter of my life had run its course.

As my conscience purged itself, the uneasiness I'd been feeling began to subside. Still, I wasn't exactly clear on how to move forward. My biggest concern was my willingness to be vulnerable to the possibility of another man loving me or hurting me. And then, in a flash, the answer came to me in an epiphany. In order to move forward, I first had to let go of the ghost of Darius Patterson. And, second, I had to give myself permission to let go of the past hurt, dysfunction, and self-doubt.

I was brought out of my reverie by the chirping noise of my cell phone's message notifier. I was so deep in thought I hadn't even noticed that the water was now lukewarm. Feeling slightly rejuvenated, I bathed, then got out the tub and dried off. My phone was on the charger on the nightstand, so I sat on the bed to check my message. It was from Seven. It read:

Hello, beautiful. Hope your week has been going well thus far. Didn't want anything, just wanted you to know you're on my mind. Peace.

His thoughtfulness made me blush. It had been years since something so simple as a text was used to show affection towards me. And I liked it. I texted back a flattered emoji.

I normally pick Yasmin up at 4pm, but on this day I picked her up at 2pm so we could hang together. We went to the mall and did a little shopping. Afterwards, we got some ice cream and went to the park so she could play with other kids. She was pooped by the time we got home. I gave her a bath and put her to bed. My mind was clear, so I opened my nightstand drawer and took out the book I was currently reading – The Disordered Cosmos by Chanda Prescod-Weinstein – and went downstairs to read and enjoy a glass of wine.

I woke up Saturday morning feeling tight from all the squats and lunges from the day before. I loved how firm and tone my butt and legs looked; it was the after-effects I didn't care for. After using the restroom, I went downstairs to get the day started with a cup of coffee.

Ever since my breakthrough, I'd been getting sufficient rest and was feeling spiritually lighter. I should have had a real conversation with myself years ago.

Surprisingly, I was looking forward to dinner with Seven, although I was unsure if he could cook. He had called me when he got back from New York to give me his address and confirm our date. The timing couldn't have been better it was Darius's weekend to have Yasmin. I contemplated what to wear while sitting on the island stool enjoying my cup of coffee.

Yasmin got out of bed, so I whipped up some scrambled eggs, hash browns, and toast. My plan was to have the house cleaned early so I could go get my nails and feet done after Darius picked Yas up.

After I finished cleaning downstairs, me and Yasmin took our baths. I dressed her in purple shorts, a cute t-shirt with a bear on the front, and purple and white Nike Air Max sneakers. I expected Darius any minute, so I threw on some fashion leggings, a white crop-top, and matching Gucci sandals and purse. I looked out the window and saw Darius pulling up.

We were on our way down the steps when the doorbell rang. I opened it, then went to collect Yasmin's favorite dolls. I put them in her bag. She was now ready to go.

"There go daddy's sweetheart!" Darius said enthusiastically, picking her up and kissing her.

As usual, Yasmin was super-excited to see her dad.

I put on my sunglasses, grabbed my purse, then handed him her bag.

"You look nice," he said.

"Thank you. So do you."

"We're going to the aquarium today. Wanna come?"

His invite threw me for a loop, considering we hadn't done anything together as a family in years. "I'll pass today. I already have plans," I replied, heading towards the door.

"Another date?" he asked in a funny tone.

I locked the door behind me, noticing the discontented look on his face. "Boy, bye," I said, walking past him to the garage.

The nerve of him, acting like he mad 'cause I got plans. Now he knows how I felt all those times I pleaded for him to do things with us, but he had 'plans.'

While driving, I found it ironic how I finally had the courage to let go of the past and move forward with my life. *And now he checkin' for me, complimenting me, and inviting me to hang wit' them.*

As anticipated, the nail salon was packed. I took a number and sat by the propped open door allowing the breeze in. Once it was my turn, I got in the massage chair and adjusted the features. I put my feet in the water and began to relax.

Minutes later, my phone started ringing. It was Hanifa.

I answered in a tranquil voice, "Hello?"

"What you into?"

"Sitting in the massage chair, soaking my feet."

"You sound like it's an orgasmic experience," she laughed.

"It's close. What up with you?"

"Just chillin'. I was thinking about going to a poetry jam and have a few drinks later. You down?"

"Sorry, boo. I can't tonight. Seven invited me to dinner at his place."

"Is he cooking or just picking up something for y'all to eat at his place?"

Excited, I answered, "He's cooking!"

"Um, sound like somebody 'bout to give up some coochie!" she teased.

"Whatever!"

"Girl, please! He fine, educated, successful, and offered to cook for you... oh, he can most definitely get it!"

Hanifa was just being her typical outspoken self.

"It's funny because I'm excited and nervous at the same time, and it's just dinner," I stated.

"Listen to me, Brooke, don't take yo' second-guessing ass over there and act stiff and nervous. That brother been on yo' line since the art gallery, so relax, be yourself, and just have a good time tonight."

"I hear you," I said, laughing. "I'll let you know tomorrow how dinner went."

"Aight. Peace."

I ended the call and went back into chill mode.

While standing in front of the closet looking for something to wear, I ran my hands through my locs. I pulled out a blue jean shirt-dress and a pair of wedge sandals. Chic, but comfortable. I put on a sexy, white thong and bra set, then sat at my vanity and styled my locs in a cute updo. This was the perfect occasion to wear the Tom Ford Bitter Peach perfume I recently purchased at the mall. I sprayed a light mist on my cleavage and wrists. I checked myself in the mirror after I got dressed. *Sexy if I must say myself.*

I pulled into the underground parking garage on East Street and stopped at the guard stand. The guard slid the window back.

"How may I help you, ma'am?"

"I'm here to see Seven Goodwin."

"He's expecting you, ma'am. You can park in space 35. Take the elevator to floor 18," he instructed while raising the guard rail.

Slowly making my way through the garage, I noticed that most of the vehicles were high-end: Bentleys, Porsches, Rolls Royces, and Mercedes Benzes. I pulled into space 35. Next to me was a black, tinted out Mercedes Benz G650. This had Seven written all over it. I pulled down my visor to apply a fresh coat of lip balm. I then checked my eyeliner and made my way to the elevator.

As it ascended, so did my anxiety. I became more nervous as the floor numbers grew and the elevator came to a stop. I took a deep breath as the doors opened. I stepped off and was immediately blown away by the high ceiling and grandeur of the interior décor. A beautifully lit electric fireplace was on the wall. I was two steps into the man's home and found myself getting moist.

Seven emerged from the kitchen wearing blue docker shorts, a blue Polo shirt, and house shoes.

"Hey, queen! You look beautiful."

"Thanks," I said, looking around. "It smells like you know what you doing in there," I smiled as we embraced in a friendly hug. He smelled so good I wouldn't have minded if it lasted longer.

The smooth sounds of Sade's *Gift of Life* played from the speakers. I followed Seven towards the kitchen, where a delectable aroma emanated from two skillets on the stove.

Sitting my purse on the granite, island counter, I asked, "What you making?"

"This evening we'll be enjoying pan-seared Mahi-Mahi, jumbo shrimp, with grilled squash and Zucchini." He made a facial expression like he knew the meal was the bomb.

His place looked like something out of a magazine. The floor-to-ceiling windows led out to a furnished terrace with panoramic views of the city. The kitchen had all stainless-steel appliances; a sleek oven vent; smart refrigerator; wine cooler; beautiful, white cabinets to match the white granite with bluish, grey veins in them; grey, stained, wooden floors throughout.

"The food will be ready shortly. Would you like something to drink? Wine, cognac, Ciroc?" he offered, then squeezed a lemon wedge on the shrimp, causing it to sizzle.

"I'll have Ciroc with pineapple juice if you have any," I said, admiring him work at the stove. He definitely knew what he was doing.

Seven walked over to the wet bar and poured me a drink. He then poured himself a glass of Hennessy XO and returned. My drink was a bit strong, but I didn't say anything. I figured it would help calm my nerves.

"This is really nice, Seven," I complimented while walking over by the window to take in the view.

"Thanks. I bought it just for the views."

The word 'bought' caught my attention. These penthouses started at $1.3 million.

"Take your shoes off and make yourself at home. There's a powder room over there if you need it," he pointed. "My office is down the hall; there's a guest room; and my room is the last room in the back."

My attention was drawn to a sitting area with built-in bookcases filled with books. I walked over to see what type of books interested him. His personal library was filled with the works of scholars and authority figures of black academia – Dr. Richard King, Ivan Van Sertima, Asa G. Hilliard, Kaba Kamene, Kobi Kambon, George G. Jackson, Cheik Anta Diop, John Henrik Clarke, and many others.

I took a sip of my drink while scanning the top shelf. I recognized a title of holy grail proportions, one I had been searching for for years, but it was always unavailable or too expensive. The last time I checked online, new copies were selling between $4000 and $7000, while used copies were averaging $1000.

"You have some rare and hard to find books," I said, in awe of many of the titles I saw.

"What book have you been looking for? I have a few contacts who might have it or can locate it for you."

I pulled the book off the shelf. "This *Tavistock Institute of Human Relations: shaping the moral, spiritual, cultural, political, and economic decline of the United States of America*," I replied.

He turned around with a surprised look on his face. "Oooh… that one might be tough, but I'll check around for you." He seemed surprised. "What you know about that?" he asked, flashing a handsome smile.

"I'm woke." I smiled back at him.

"A wise man once said, 'A man's mind is elevated to the status of the woman with whom he associates.'"

"Alexandre Dumas," I quipped, acknowledging the renown, English-born, black man who wrote The Three Musketeers.

I made my way down to his office. It was sleek and extravagant like the rest of his penthouse, which was no surprise. There was a glass-top desk with a large monitor and keyboard on it and several nice chairs. On the walls were pictures of notable, black men. He had one of John Carlos and Tommy Stanton's iconic Olympic pose with their fists raised, wearing black, leather gloves. He also had pictures of Dr. King, Malcolm X, John Henrik Clarke, Marcus Garvey, Muhammad Ali, Fred Hampton and Huey P. Newton, and Earth, Wind & Fire, to name a few.

Seven was preparing our plates when I returned.

"I love your office," I said, following him out on the terrace.

"Thanks. I call it the Black Room."

"Why the Black Room?"

"Because it's a space where I can sit and just unplug from second-frequency people. I look at those great men and tap into the frequency of the ancestors and aspire to their level of greatness," he stated with conviction. "Try this," he said, offering me a fork of shrimp.

My tastebuds exploded when I ate it off the fork. "Yeah, you can cook," I admitted, giving him props.

The vibe at that moment was perfect. The sunset was slowly waning. I had a nice buzz going. The food was amazing. Our conversation was intellectually stimulating. We flirted back and forth using seductive eye contact, and also shared a few good laughs.

"I gotta give it to you, dinner was wonderful. Thank you."

"You're welcome, beautiful. Hopefully, you'll let me do it more often." His eyes were filled with lust. They told me everything he wanted me to know.

We went back inside. I replenished our glasses while he rinsed the dishes and loaded them into the dishwasher. This time, my drink was perfect.

The illumination of the electric fireplace, along with the soft music, created a cozy atmosphere. I nestled up in the corner of the sofa. Jill Scott's *He Loves Me* was playing. The lyrics perfectly described the way I felt.

Seven came and joined me on the sofa. He took a sip of his drink and sat it on the table. He looked like he had a plan.

"Give'em here," he said, motioning with his hands for my feet.

I repositioned myself and put my feet in his hands. While his strong, well-manicured fingers gripped my feet, his thumbs massaged my soles.

Staring at me, he said, "You have pretty feet."

"Thank you," I softly replied, reaching for my drink. His touch was causing my body to undergo the heightened sensations I felt every time I was around him – elevated heart rate, butterflies, increased wetness.

"So, Ms. Collins, have you given any thought to where you are at this point in your life?"

The moment of truth had arrived. I felt nervous all of a sudden, so I took a deep breath. "As a matter of fact, I have." Looking at him, I continued, "I can honestly say I am no longer trapped in the past. I'm focused on moving forward with my life and being emotionally available for the right man. A man who wants to get to know me better, build with me, and love me," I amorously stated.

"I'm that man, queen."

"Are you?"

Convincingly, he affirmed, "Absolutely."

Seizing the moment, he sat my drink on the table, scooted closer, and kissed me. I was hesitant. It had been years since I felt a man's lips on mine, let alone someone other than Darius's. his lips were soft and supple. The passion raging in his eyes incited me to react, so I leaned in and initiated the next kiss, smacking as I tasted his tongue.

My sexual urge overrode my voice of reason as our tongues intertwined. I straddled his lap and began helping him take his shirt off. He raised his arms and I pulled it over his head and tossed it. His chest was chiseled like a sculpted piece of art.

He untied the belt around my waist, and I pulled the dress over my head and tossed it on top of his shirt. He unclasped my bra, and I discarded it. My breasts and hard nipples were fully exposed. He put them up to his mouth. The softness of his lips and tongue as he kissed, licked, and sucked on my nipples sent chills all over my body. "Uaaah!" I moaned in delight.

Seven knew just how to touch me, excite me, and tease me. My body was on fire. "You smell so damn good," he moaned as he switched nipples. The sensation was so stimulating that I panted heavily as I felt myself cum. In all of my years, I had never been brought to an orgasm from a man simply sucking my titties. It felt amazing.

My initial thought of him being single because he probably had a small dick quickly disappeared as I felt the growing mound beneath me. Eager to release years of pent-up energy, I unfastened his shorts, then slid down between his legs to help him out of his shorts and boxers. Before my eyes was nothing less than an act from God. I wasn't sure if I was just tipsy or seeing things. His dick was at least nine or ten inches long, thick, and straight as an arrow with a bell-shaped head.

During college, I had encountered a guy or two with a big dick, but nothing remotely close to this. Although I was a little intimidated, I was excited that my long sex drought was about to end.

I caressed it with both hands, admiring it before inserting it into my mouth and giving it a deep suck. I slowly retracted and swirled my tongue around the supple head. It had been years since I sucked on a dick, and this was definitely one I wanted to give a good try.

Taking my time, I licked up and down the shaft with the flat of my tongue. Next, I sucked on his balls one at a time, then the sensitive area just below them. His dick frolicked as it got harder. I slowly licked my way back to the head and began bobbing up and down as I stroked and rolled my hand grip on it. "Ooh, shit," he moaned, caressing the back of my neck.

I'd fantasized about freaking with a man like this for so long that I didn't mind the overflow of saliva leaking out of my mouth and running down my chin. I sucked like a woman possessed. Overwhelmed, Seven stopped me.

"Hold on, Brooke," he panted. "That feels so damn good you got me 'bout to cum already. Let this sensation subside a little."

At that moment, H-Town's *They Like It Slow* came on. I was unsure how his playlist seemed to know what songs to play, for it played all the right songs at the right time.

Seven sat me on the couch and knelt between my legs. He started kissing me, forcing me to lay back on the pillow. Anticipation streamed through me as he slowly kissed his way down my body. He latched on the waistband of my panties, and I raised up so he could pull them down. I stepped out of them. Without hesitation, he pushed my legs back and kissed my pussy lips. I melted into the pillows.

His tongue traced my lips then went inside of me with such skill and precision that I screamed, begging him not to stop as multiple orgasms rippled through my body. Thankfully, he stopped. I needed him to because the room was spinning, and I was seeing stars.

Suddenly, I felt him teasing my sopping, wet pussy with the tip of his dick. And then he slowly entered me. My walls began expanding to accommodate him until I was overwhelmed.

"Shit!" I yelled, bracing his waist. "It's been a long time since I had sex, or anything as big as you, so you gotta be gentle wit' me," I pleaded.

"I gotchu, baby," he said, then kissed me.

I knew my pussy was tight, but I didn't expect to feel like a bornagain virgin having sex for the very first time.

Seven was a gentleman. He took his time, stroking in and out at a pace and depth that was enjoyable. His stroke allowed my pussy to adapt to being stretched to new dimensions. Once I got comfortable, I started moving in sync with him.

"Damn, Brooke... you feel so good, baby," he professed, slowly going deeper.

I hadn't felt that wanted, desired, and appreciated in years, and it was obvious because my body received his deep thrusts with unbridled pleasure.

"Fuck me, Seven... Fuck me!" I begged as I felt another orgasm building up.

He picked up the pace, and the sensation intensified. With each stroke, I felt his balls smacking my asshole.

"Oh my, God… baby, baby, babyyy!" I screamed as my legs shuddered uncontrollably from another exhilarating orgasm.

As he came, he pushed so deep inside of me that it snatched my breath away. I wrapped my arms around his neck and pulled him into my body as I held on for dear life. I had never been fucked so hard for so long, and I loved every damn second of it.

The light energy of the morning sun rays shone on my face and caused me to open my eyes. I was in an unfamiliar bed in an unfamiliar room. The clock on the nightstand showed 8:45am. When or how I ended up there was unclear to me, for the last thing I remembered was us cummin' together on the couch before I passed out.

I needed to pee but didn't want to move because I was so comfortable. I rolled over. Seven was on his back still asleep. I stared in awe. Even when sleep he gave me butterflies.

My curiosity got the better of me. I raised the sheet to see if what I saw last night was real or if my mind was playing tricks on me. I peeped. It was real! Even when flaccid, his dick looked juicy.

No longer able to control my bladder, I quietly slipped out of the bed and went to the bathroom, closing the door behind me. The heated floors and toilet seats were worth their weight in gold. I sat there taking in the opulence of his master suite: granite counter with double vanity sinks; a beautiful, frosted glass encased to a marble-tiled shower; touch-screen, adjustable shower features with a 24" shower head; and a huge, spa-like, soaker tub.

While washing my hands in the sink, I saw my naked reflection in the mirror and a sudden wave of guilt overcame me. It wasn't because I was intimate with someone other than my husband, but that I'd been a whole freak with him like he was my husband.

When I opened the door, I saw that Seven was awake. The sheet, barely covering his lower extremities, exposed his sexy, chocolate chest and arms. He stared at my body with wanton, sparkling eyes as I walked back to the bed.

"Good morning, queen."

"Good morning."

"How you feeling?"

"You trying to be funny?" I asked with threatening eyes.

"Not at all," he answered, flashing a big smile.

He pulled the sheet back, inviting me in. I climbed in and nestled against his body. My head lay on his chest.

"I asked because you said it's been a while since you had sex, and I wanted it to be as good to you as it was for me."

"My girl," I said, referring to my pussy, "is a little swollen, but you were amazing!" I kissed his chest.

"As were you, baby." He paused. "Brooke, I don't want to pressure you into anything, I just want you to know I'm sincere about what I said last night. You're special, and I'm hoping we can be exclusive."

The sound of the words 'special' and 'exclusive' made my heart skip a beat. "You're special, too, Seven. But us being exclusive is the only option for me if we move forward. You should know my divorce isn't finalized yet, but it should be any day now. And keep in mind I have a daughter."

"None of that is an issue with me. It'll be finalized when it's finalized. As for your daughter, I know you're a mom first, so whenever you're comfortable with me meeting her, I look forward to it."

As I rubbed his chest, I noticed the ever-growing bulge of his dick protruding through the sheets. Fully aware of what was beneath it, I slid my hand under the sheet and fondled it, feeling the monstrosity of it throbbing in my hand as I slowly stroked it.

"Umm-um," I sighed in awe. "You should know this is a lot of dick to work with, right?"

"Just a little bit," he modestly said.

"No. A lot!"

"Keep doing what you doing and you gon' find yourself in trouble."

"Good trouble is necessary," I seductively stated.

"Well, let me show you how to work with it."

He rolled me over onto my stomach and positioned himself between my legs. He slowly kissed my spine, then began sucking on the back of my neck. I turned my face on the pillow and anxiously waited for him to enter me. He rubbed the head on my wetness until it made splashing noises. "Yeah, that's what I'm talking 'bout right there. Now she ready," he said, satisfied with my juicy pussy.

He entered me. I instantly tensed up. "Uaaahh," I moaned as my walls expanded. His stroke was tempered and tender. I rolled my pelvis in small circles, to which he enjoyed.

"That's right, show me you can work with it, Brooke," he said in a sultry tone, spanking my cheeks one after the other. "Can you handle it, baby?"

It was feeling so good I could barely speak. "Yesss," I answered in a low moan.

"Do you want all of it, baby?"

"Yesss, I want all of it."

"Well, show me you want all of it."

I slowly raised up onto my hands and knees and began bucking back against his big dick. He matched me stroke for stroke.

"Get it, Brooke... get it, Brooke," he cheered.

I looked over my shoulder at him. "You like that?"

"Hell yeah! Look at that juicy booty bouncin'!"

He spanked both of my cheeks once more, then grabbed my hips and increased the pace. I could tell he was on the verge of cummin'. With each stroke, he hit my spot, causing me to let out 'aaahs' and 'ooohs' in a loud falsetto.

"Look at all that on my dick! Ssss... uhhhh," he groaned as he exploded.

I collapsed onto the bed, swooning from pleasure. As he withdrew, my pussy leaked like a running faucet. His sheets, needless to say, were soaked. I closed my eyes and was out like a light.

Chapter 6

(Hanifa)

Sunday mornings were the most peaceful times in our house. This was all due to the kids having stayed up late the night before, and because Jahsani always slept in. I used these moments as opportunities to get in a little me-time. On this particular Sunday, I got up and rolled a joint, then went downstairs to the kitchen to make a hot cup of tea with ginger and turmeric. I opened the backdoor and walked out into the backyard barefoot. I liked feeling the earth's electrical pulse when inspecting the garden.

Growing up, my grandmother and mother taught me the importance of being able to work the land and produce quality food to ensure my family never went hungry or ate unhealthily. Grandma used to say, "Your medicine is not what you have in your bathroom cabinet, it's what you have in your refrigerator." She lived to be 101 years of age.

It was another beautiful morning. The temperature was around 70° and expected to reach the upper eighties. I fired up the joint and sipped the hot tea. My herbs were sprouting well. The tomatoes were turning red, and the cucumbers, peppers, and mustard greens were in full bloom. Once I finished smoking, I got the water hose and sprayed the soil while performing libations to the ancestors.

Feeling relaxed and in a mellow mood mentally, the last thing I needed was for the kids to wake up and kill my vibe, so I headed inside and got started on breakfast. The savory aroma of scrambled, cheese eggs, salmon croquette patties, fried potatoes with onions and peppers, and biscuits permeating the house woke everyone up. Like an army of ants, they filed into the kitchen one by one.

"Good morning, baby," Jahsani greeted me, opening the refrigerator and taking out the orange juice.

"Morning, baby."

I fixed the kids' plates first. Once they were situated, I fixed mine's and Jahsani's. I then joined them at the table. Having everyone at the table for breakfast and dinner was quality time Jahsani and I both enjoyed. This was usually when we got an earful of the tv shows the kids liked, an update on video game characters, or who did what to who. There was never a dull moment with Jahlil and Jahlissa. One minute they were best friends and getting along, the next they were at each other's throat. It was a constant battle for individuality with them.

Jahsani collected everyone's plate once we were finished. He rinsed them off and began putting them in the dishwasher.

"What you got up for today, baby" he asked.

I was sitting at the table watching Jahlil play his handheld Nintendo game. "Michaela asked me to go look at a couple of houses with her this afternoon. What you got planned?"

"Nothing! I'm gon' kick back and chillax. I was thinking we could take the kids to get ice cream later on when the sun goes down."

Jahlil and Jahlissa were excited.

"Sounds good to me. You still want me to oil your scalp later?"

"Yeah, but right now I got something else you can oil for me," he covertly said with his 'It's Mr. Nasty Time' facial expression.

With the kids always around, we learned to speak in code to throw them off the trail of grown folks' business.

"Ummm.... Well, I'm 'bout to go get in the shower so I can be ready when Michaela gets here," I coyly stated, patting him on the butt as he cleaned the stove.

"Don't meet me there, beat me there!" he replied as I walked away throwing up the deuces.

As soon as I walked in the bedroom, I went in the bathroom and turned on the shower to let it steam up. I stripped naked, brushed my teeth, then wet my face and applied an exfoliating mask.

While looking in the closet for something to wear, Jahsani walked in. "I'm right in time!" he gleefully remarked, staring at me.

"Can I at least wipe off my mask?" I asked, laughing at how thirsty he sounded.

"Nope. Ain't no telling how long we got. I want you right now, right here," he said, positioning me on the edge of the bed so he could hit it from behind standing up.

He quickly pulled his wife-beater off, and then his shorts. I spread my knees and dipped low, resting on my forearms, readying myself. He spanked my right cheek. I felt the tip of his dick teasing up and down my pussy, getting me wet. Seconds later, he pushed inside of me, and currents of pleasure coursed through me.

"Uaaah, yes!" I moaned.

The pace, rhythm, and stroke pattern felt like he was casually walking in my pussy. Shallow strokes. Slow, deep, upward strokes. Fluid, long strokes. Each one strummed along my clit and caused me to bite my bottom lip to refrain from screaming his name.

"How that feel, queen?"

"Oooh!" I purred as I started cummin'.

"Yeah... give it to me, Nifa!" he replied, watching me bathe his dick in my nectar.

"I'm giving it to you, baby," I moaned. "Go deeper, Jahsani,"

He increased the pace and began going deeper to the point the loud clapping sound of his pelvis pounding against my cheeks could be heard over the shower.

I could feel the big one building up as his balls bounced off my clit with each stroke. The sensation of ecstasy was stronger than my willpower to not be loud.

"Oh, baby... right there... keep it right there!" I pleaded.

Out of nowhere, *Bam! Bam! Bam!* There were three knocks on the door. "MOM, TELL JAHLIL TO LEAVE ME ALONE!"

The banging startled us and interrupted my eruption. We paused for a second. We were extra quiet... but not for too long.

Jahsani quickly returned to the previous pace and depth, and the tingling sensation returned. I reached underneath my body and began massaging his balls as he continued stroking. His groans got louder, so I knew he was close to exploding, too.

"Get it, Jahsani... this yo' pussy, baby... this yo' pussy!" I buried my face into a pillow to muffle my screams as my orgasm unleashed itself.

Bam! Bam! Bam! Three more knocks at the door. "MOM, TELL JAHLISSA TO STAY OUT MY ROOM!"

I was in the throes of ecstasy and in no shape to play referee to their latest melee.

"Y'ALL AIN'T GON' LIKE IT IF I HAVE TO COME OUT THERE!" I shouted.

Jahsani thought it was funny. "You know good and well you ain't gon' buss a grape," he said, laughing at my idle threat while massaging the globes of my ass, enjoying his nut.

He was right, but that was beside the point. "I ain't gon' buss what?" I repeated, disconnecting from him and turning around. "I bet I buss this, tho!" I put his dick in my mouth and began sucking it.

"Good God Almighty!" he said in a hushed tone, his knees buckling.

I watched his abs contract over and over as the sensitive sensation sent currents of pleasure coursing through his body until he could no longer take it. He pushed my head away and collapsed on the bed. I got up and went to get in the shower.

As the hot water beat down on my body, I closed my eyes and allowed the high of the morning's romp to settle in. the shower door suddenly opened and Jahsani stepped in with his locs down by his chest. The sight of his body made me horny all over again.

We switched out so he could wet his body under the shower head. I rubbed and massaged his deltoids and shoulders as the water cascaded onto his head and down his body. I slipped my arms under his and rested my face against his back while holding his chest, appreciative of the man, father, and husband he was.

We switched out again. Letting the water beat on my back, I grabbed his dick and slowly stroked it, trying to get it back up. The love and affection radiating in his languid eyes were heartfelt. He kissed me, then started sucking on my neck while gripping my booty, kneading it with his fingers.

The softness of his lips and tongue sucking on my nipples reignited my sexual urges. He nudged my left knee with his, then lifted it up with his hand and put my foot on top of the soap dish. This was why we always had to get it reglued.

He kissed down my body until he was on one knee before my pearly gate. I braced myself against the wall with one hand as he kissed, licked, then stuck his tongue inside me. I delightfully moaned and caressed the back of his head, coaxing his tongue to go deeper.

Seeing my desire for more, he inserted two fingers into my pussy and stroked them while flickering his tongue on my clit, taking me over the edge. "Yesss, Jahsani! Yesss!" I let out as he brought me to climax.

As I stood there engulfed in the rapture of the sensation, he lathered up a rag and began washing the front of my body and feet. It was simple things like this that made me want to move heaven and earth to give him peace of mind. We switched out again. I lathered up a rag and washed him up. When I finished, I kissed the tip of his dick and got out so he could have a moment alone.

One of the luxuries of wearing my hair natural was that it didn't take hours doing it. I lotioned up, put on a black panty and bra set, then picked out my afro.

At 1pm, the sound of a horn honking twice came from the driveway. I peeked out the window and saw Michaela's pewtercolored Porsche truck outside. Beaming with energy from my morning exploits, I descended the porch steps, did a double pirouette, then strolled over to the driveway to get in.

"What's up, gorgeous?" I greeted Michaela as I clicked my seat belt.

"Oh, lord. Aren't you just full of energy today. Jahsani must've realigned yo' spine," she joked.

"Don't hate 'cause my man puts it downnn!"

"At least one of us getting broke off on a regular." She backed out of the driveway. "Girl, the other day I had to pull up at Carl's job and finesse him out the dick. Like, c'mon now. I know he working 16-hour days to help with the down payment, but I told him I could handle it if it means we see more of each other."

"I hear you, sis, but you gotta allow him to be a man. And in his mind that means being able to provide, protect, and have a voice in the relationship. Carl know you can handle the down payment, but if you emasculate him over financial matters, I promise you, you gon' regret it because y'all relationship gon' go in the opposite direction."

"I hear you," she said dejectedly. "It's crazy how when women getting the bag we gotta cater to they ego, but when a man got the bag they can do whatever they want." She shook her head.

"Nah, sis. Men who think having money gives them the right to be controlling, disrespectful, and irresponsible aren't men at all. It's about balance. Teamwork makes the dream work."

"I'm not saying Carl is like that, but men in general... I just feel like, if I got it, we got it! I'm gon' hold my man down and I expect for him to hold me down, and together we gon' make it do what it do."

"All I'm saying is be patient, Michaela. I haven't seen you this happy before, and I can tell y'all love each other. If you wanna get yo' spine realigned, figure out when he's available and make it happen."

The first open house was in an established subdivision in College Park. As we pulled up to the house, a couple with kids were walking up to the door. Houses in this area didn't stay on the market long due to the good school district, accessibility to the freeways, shopping centers, and parks.

Michaela opened the door. The beautiful, pine wood floors stood out as soon as we walked in. The house was recently renovated but lacked the open floor plan and finishes she was looking for. We toured the house for fifteen minutes, then left and headed to the next one.

I assured her that finding the right house that checked off most, if not all, of their must-haves was going to be a process she had to be patient with. Jahsani and I looked at over 20 houses before we found our home.

"Have y'all decided on how to celebrate y'all ten-year anniversary?" she enthusiastically asked.

"Not really. I'm thinking of hiring an event planner and throwing something at the house in the backyard, so I might need you to hook me up with someone reputable.

"I gotchu."

My phone started ringing. It was Brooke. Eager to know how her dinner went, I answered right away.

"Hey, luv!" I put her on speakerphone. "I got you on speakerphone. How was dinner with Mr. Chocolate?" I asked with genuine excitement.

"Girrrl... where you at?"

The level of consternation in her voice fanned the flames of my desire to know. "I'm out house-hunting with the sexually frustrated Michaela 'the Body' Jackson," I joked.

Michaela chimed in. "Whatever. Hi, Brooke."

"What's up?" replied Brooke, laughing. "How long y'all gon' be out?"

"We're headed to Jonesborough to look at a house, and that's it."

"Y'all might as well swing by here when you leave there since you gon' be on my side of town."

"Aight. See you in a little."

"Peace."

Michaela turned up the volume to Ari Lennox's song *Bussit* and accelerated the Porsche truck down 285. She got off on Campbellton Road and headed east for a few miles until we came upon an area of houses under construction. Most of the houses were cookie-cutter, two-story homes with attached two-car garages, a small patch of grass in the front, and neighbors within an earshot of hearing her pass gas. It was not what she was looking for, but we came too far not to look inside.

The entrance of the house opened into a nice foyer with a high ceiling, making a grand statement. To the left was a big front room that led to a dining room. We turned right and walked into a nice kitchen with all new stainless-steel appliances, a six-range gas stove, and a bonus space off to the side. She liked what she saw.

But as we headed up the stairs, Michaela pointed out a dealbreaker. The master bedroom was directly in front of the stairwell. I understood why she didn't like it, especially since she wanted kids someday. The last thing you want is for everyone in the house to hear you getting it in whenever they go up or down the stairs. We headed back to the truck and headed to go see Brooke.

Brooke opened the door barefooted, wearing leopard-print tights, a wife-beater, and her locs wrapped in a black, silk scarf.

"Y'all want something to drink?" asked Brooke, strolling towards the kitchen.

"What you sippin' on?" Michaela inquired.

"Gatorade. A sister gotta hydrate after last night."

"Whaaat!" I replied, mouth wide open from excitement. "Grab two glasses and a bottle of Mascoto because I want all the tea."

Michaela reached up in the cabinet and retrieved two goblets while Brooke handed me the bottle of wine. The three of us walked over into the family room and got comfortable on the sofa.

"Was I right?" I asked, smiling while Michaela poured the wine. "You gave'em some, didn't you?"

Brooke covered her face with her hands and nodded. "You were right, Nifa, but let me explain what happened," she said with a smirk on her face. "So, he lives downtown on the 18th floor of the towers…"

Michaela cut her off. "Hold up. The Towers? Shiid, ol' boy selling more than art if he staying up in there. Thems million-dollar penthouses!"

"Facts!" I added, taking a sip of wine.

Brooke continued. "He used to design shopping malls, and he still invests in commercial real estate. Anyway, like I was saying, soon as I stepped off the elevator, my heart skipped two beats and I was ready to come out my panties then!" she laughed. "It looked like I walked into a home on the cover of Architectural Design. Sade was playing in the background, and the aroma in the air smelled so good… he pan-seared Mahi Mahi, jumbo shrimp, grilled squash and zucchini."

"Damn, girl!" blurted out Michaela. "I would've gave him some coochie, too!"

"Nifa, his mind and energy is sooo beautiful! The connection we have is so refreshing and strong. And you would love his library. He got books that are so rare and hella expensive. I was shocked to see several titles he had."

"Books like what?" I asked, curious to know what she deemed rare.

"Girl, he got that *Tavistock Institute: Human Relations, GAGUT (God Almighty, Grand Unified Theorem)* by Dr. Gabriel Oyibo; *The Star of Deep Beginnings* by Dr. Charles Finch," she said, naming a few.

"Yeah, he definitely got exclusive literature," I stated.

"I had a couple of glasses of Ciroc, he was drinking Hennessy XO. We ate on the terrace, talked, joked, laughed, and just had a good time. Once it got dark, we went inside and chilled on the sofa in front of the electric fireplace. We started kissing..."

Brooke's facial expression changed, and her eyes looked out into the distance like she was reliving the moment.

"... his lips were so soft and moist, and before I knew it we were naked on the couch."

"Um hmm," I sighed, sensing she was holding out on us. "Was the dick good? Yes or naw?"

"Oh, my God... y'all, the man is a living, breathing poster child of the black man legend – he's big, thick, and long. At least nine or ten inches of full-blooded Mandingo stock," she said, reveling in the recollection of his manhood.

"Yesss, Seven! Yesss!" cheered Michaela. "Wait, did he know how to operate all that equipment? Ain't nothing more disappointing than a man with a big dick and whack sex."

"Facts," I added.

"Now, y'all know I ain't been with a man in damn near two years. Girl, why he make me cum just from sucking my titties! He ate my pussy so good the room started spinning and I was in that muthafucka seeing stars!"

"I'm officially team Seven," Michaela said, holding up her glass as to declare allegiance.

"But once he put it in, I swear, I thought he split my coochie wide open," said Brooke as her eyes rolled in the back of her head.

"I know exactly what you mean, girl," said Michaela. "Carl's dick is huge, too, and every time we have sex it feels like he stretching my kitty kat out the frame."

"Last thing I remembered was the room spinning and seeing stars, then I woke up this morning in his bed. I don't know when or how I got there, but that's where I woke up at."

"Damn, Brooke," I said in awe, "that sounds like a helluva night!"

"So, if you spent the night that means you got that morning dick, too," teased Michaela. "I'm telling y'all, that morning dick hit differently."

"Facts!" I emphatically stated at the thought of my morning experience. All of a sudden, the joy and excitement in Brooke's eyes disappeared. Concerned, I asked, "What's wrong, Brooke?"

"As I was washing my hands this morning, I saw the reflection of my naked body in the mirror and felt guilty for having slept with someone other than my husband."

"What!?!" me and Michaela shouted simultaneously.

"Wait, wait, wait," I repeated, shaking my head in disbelief. "You mean to tell me you got a man with a third leg laying in the bed and you trippin' off of Darius's cheating ass? Please tell me you joking."

Brooke shrugged her shoulders.

It was no secret to us all what she endured over the years with Darius, from being stressed, depressed, and on the verge of having a nervous breakdown, so I wasn't going to get on her too bad.

Michaela sat her drink on the coffee table. "But, Brooke, just the other day you told me you were ready to move on from Darius emotionally. What happened?"

Tears began to well up in her eyes. "I don't know why I felt guilty, but part of me does," she said with a blank look on her face.

"I'll tell you why," I said, sitting my glass on the table, "it's completely understandable that your conscience kicked in. You haven't been with anyone else other than Darius in the past seven years. You're use to him. It's going to take some time to get use to a different man," I explained.

"That makes sense," agreed Michaela.

"So, what's the deal with you and Seven, or was that a one time thing? I know you ain't a fan of community dick," I inquired as Brooke wiped her eyes.

"He wants to be exclusive."

"And how do you feel about that?"

She took a deep breath to regain her composure. "I'm flattered. Y'all know I wanna be with a man who wants to love and appreciate me as much as I do him, and Seven seems like that kind of man."

"Sis, you spoke that energy into the universe, and now it has manifested in your life, so what you gon' do? Are you gon' reject your blessing, or are you gon' nurture it and grow with it?"

"I'm going to nurture it," Brooke answered in a hopeful tone.

Michaela broke up the counseling session. "I'm glad you said that because now I know you ain't lost yo' damn mind. It ain't every day you meet a man like him, especially with a dick that big, so allow me to put you up on game. Keep the Epson Salt under the bathroom sink. It'll keep you from having to run downstairs to get it to put in your bath, 'cause it's many swollen nights ahead of you, trust and believe!"

Chapter 7

(Michaela)

Wednesday's workout was more intense than I intended it to be. We were on the stair master doing the HIT (high intensity training) routine. Sweat poured from our foreheads. Our sports bras were soaked. Brooke's thighs and glutes were on fire, but she pushed through it. As for me, I was so tense from being sexually deprived that I didn't feel the effects like her.

"Keep climbing, Brooke! Two more minutes," I instructed, breathing heavily.

This was the part most people didn't like - the grind, the hard work, and the dedication it takes to maintain a curvaceous, toned physique. Staying fit had been a priority of mine since my days in college, and old habits are hard to break.

As the timer on the monitor started flashing, I counted it down out loud, *8, 7, 6, 5, 4, 3, 2, good job, Brooke!* I then got off.

"Whew!" Brooke exhaled in a sigh of relief, breathing heavily. "What in the hell got into you?" she asked as we got on the treadmill to do a ten-minute cool-down.

"I got so much on my mind and going hard in the gym is how I blow off steam." I squirted some water into my mouth.

"Well, next time you wanna act like you climbing the stairway to heaven, please let me know the day before so I can keep my ass at home!" she joked. "Seriously, tho', are you good?"

"I'm aight. It's just, I'm trying hard to find the perfect house for us, and then there's work, plus we not spending enough time together because he working so much overtime... not to mention trying to figure out what to do for his 42nd birthday next month."

"I hear you girl. Looking for the perfect house is tedious work, but eventually you'll find the one for y'all. Just be patient," she said before squirting a small amount of water into her mouth. "Do you know those two guys over there staring at us?"

I followed her eyes over to the dumbbell rack. I recognized the two onlookers, then waved them off, politely dismissing them. "Girl, you know the gym the new club. Them bustas stalk every chick that come in here with some ass and titties."

We finished our cool-down and then sat on a bench for a minute.

"What you thinking about doing for his birthday?"

"I was thinking about inviting y'all to join us at Hal's Steak House for dinner, or since it's summertime, maybe we could all take a three-day trip to Jamaica."

"Girl, I can already see me before the beautiful ocean, eating good food, chilling on the beach with a drink, listening to reggae music." Ardently, she said, "I'm down. I could definitely use the getaway."

"I'll check online and see who has the best package deal, then I'll let y'all know."

While driving home, I thought about what Hanifa said about nothing kills a relationship quicker than pride and money issues. My relationship with Carl was the best I'd ever experienced, so the last thing I wanted was to push him away because I made more money than he did.

With the idea of taking a trip for Carl's birthday fresh on my mind, I jumped online as soon as I walked in the house. Due to it being peak season, most agencies were offering similar prices for the same package. I scrolled down and came across an ad for a three-day, three-night, all inclusive stay at the five-star Sandals Beachfront Resort in Negril, Jamaica. Our flight would depart Friday at 7am. We'd head back to the States Monday at 6am.

Ready to get out of my wet clothes, I saved the travel agent's information, then went and got in the shower so I could get ready for my hair appointment with Carmen. After showering, I ate a turkey club sandwich. I then put on some black shorts, a white and black t-shirt with the words Melanated Queen on the front, and my favorite white and black, patent-leather Jordan XI. I grabbed a smoothie out of the refrigerator and left.

As usual, Carmen was sitting in her chair waiting on me when I entered the salon.

"What up, chica?" I greeted her.

"How you doing, Michaela?" she replied as we embraced.

"I'm good," I answered, sitting in the chair. "What you got going on?"

"Same ol', same ol'. Another day, another bill to pay," she chuckled.

"What you said," I agreed.

She buttoned the apron around my neck, then started combing my hair. "We doing the same thing to it?"

"Yeah. I sweat so much at the gym, my hair be threw in four days, so I'm keeping it as simple as possible."

"I ain't mad at you. I need to take my butt to the gym with you so I can get this baby weight off of me." She grabbed her sides and thighs.

"Me and Brooke go in the mornings, so you're more than welcome to join us."

"Let me see if I can find someone to keep the baby for me during that time."

"Before I forget, I'm pulling together a couples' trip to Jamacia for Carl's birthday next month. Would you like to go?"

"Hell yeah!" she emphatically exclaimed, spinning the chair around so I could see her. "Them kids and they damn daddies driving me crazy. Just let me know what it cost and when we leaving." She turned me back around.

"I gotchu."

Carmen suddenly became super-excited and spun the chair back around. "Oooh, Michaela... you ain't gon' believe who I ran into and was asking for your number."

"Who?"

She stood back and shifted her weight to one leg in a sassy pose and twirled the comb. "Dee Dee! Me and a few girls went to happy hour at that new strip club over by the west end shopping center, and I saw him there."

Donald "Dee Dee" Dixon was an ex-boyfriend of mine from back in the day. He helped me stay in college after all my grants and financial aid ran out. We were together for three years until he had a baby on me. He caught a ten-year federal bid for money laundering after that.

"That's good he's out of prison," I nonchalantly stated.

"Girl, quit frontin' like you don't care. That used to be yo' boo!"

"Exactly! Used to be! I'm good with the man I got now."

"Aight. I wouldn't dare give your number out without you saying to, but I did tell him he could catch you here today around this time." She smiled guiltily. "Sorry."

"It's all good. We gon' always be cool, but I ain't fucking with him like that."

She was right. I used to be head over heels in love with Dee Dee. At that time, he introduced me to the hottest promoters in Atlanta, and taught me the night life hustle. Part of me hoped he came by. I kept one eye on the door while Carmen did my hair.

An hour later, Carmen handed me a mirror and slowly turned the chair so I could check out my hair. It was cute. I got out the chair, pulled the money from my purse to pay her, then we hugged.

"See you next week. I'll call you later," I promised while heading toward the door.

"Aight. Be safe."

I was about to open my driver's door when a white, Rolls Royce Wraith blocked me in. The driver's door opened, and Dee Dee stepped out.

"Pound Cakes!" he called out, smiling from ear to ear. "I see some things never change because you're still fine."

"Hi, Dee Dee," I blushingly responded as we embraced.

Even after being in prison for a decade, he still looked and smelled good. He still had a little weight on him, but that never bothered me. It just made lying up under him more comfortable. He still had swag and boss mannerisms.

"How've you been, sweetheart?" he asked.

"Good. When you get out?"

"Eight months ago."

Looking at his car, I said, "I see you ridin' good!"

"Anything less than the best would be uncivilized," he candidly replied. "We just opened a shake joint on the westside. You should come through and let me buy you a drink some time."

"I might."

"I been trying to get a line on you, but Carmen wouldn't give me your number. I would love to take you to dinner tonight and play catch up."

"I can't. I'm in a relationship, and you know I don't play them type of games," I said with a playful smirk on my face, reminding him of the past.

"Yeah, I know. Tell you what," he said, reaching in his wallet and handing me his new card. "If you change your mind, or need me, don't hesitate to gimme a holla. It was good seeing you, Pound Cakes!"

Giving him a hug, I said, "You, too."

He got back in his Wraith and drove off. I got back in my truck and sat still for a minute to calm my nerves. Seeing him after all this time elevated my heart rate and made me think about all the good times we shared together... not to mention the sex was great. Dee Dee was the guy I came to know my body with sexually. He was the first guy I ever squirted on, 69ed with, had sex in a car and outside with, and my only threesome experience.

The brief journey down memory lane made me hot and bothered. Luckily, my hand turned over the ignition so I could leave before I gave his invitation a second thought and end up doing something I'd later regret.

When I got home, I called the travel agent and she informed me of all the resort offered and agreed to make the reservation for our dinner party on the beach. My next move was to let the girls know the price.

I called the girls individually and told them the price. Everyone was okay with it, so I called the agent back and charged the deposit on my credit card.

With thoughts of Dee Dee and the trip on my mind, I couldn't focus on work, so I logged into the chat Carmen told me about. Boy, was she right! The things being posted were on another level of freaky and outside my ideas of what is pleasurable, so I scrolled along.

I stopped on a conversation in progress. Several chicks were talking about putting Listerine strips or Halls cough drops in their mouths and allowing them to dissolve on their tongues before giving head. Once the menthol activates, it causes the skin to heat up or cool down, depending on what is used. It was interesting, to say the least.

I continued to scroll down the page. Some other chicks were talking about something called a cream pie. This is for girls who don't like the taste of semen. They said to bypass the taste, deepthroat the dick right before it explodes. Doing this allows the cum to go on down without upsetting one's tastebuds. One chick even broke down the health benefits of swallowing semen like she was a doctor. Who knew It is packed with so many enzymes, minerals, and vitamins that provide optimal health benefits?

After playing around on the chat for a while, I viewed the latest listing my realtor emailed me. Before long, I had tired myself out. I tossed and turned all night thinking about old sexcapades with Dee Dee, and more recently with Carl. Although they were two different styles of lovers, both were extremely enjoyable.

The sun was coming up, and I couldn't go another second with suppressing my sexual cravings. I got up, took a quick shower, put on some clothes, and drove to Carl's townhome. We had keys to each other's place, so I let myself in.

I laid naked in his bed waiting for him to come home. I could feel his presence and energy from his body's imprint in the mattress. His scent was trapped in the sheets and pillowcases. It was comforting, like wearing one of his shirts.

I heard the jingling of keys as they were placed on the dining room table. He walked into the bedroom. When his tired-looking eyes saw me sprawled across the bed naked, they got big as paper plates, and so was the smile on his face.

"My, my, my... only God could create something so beautiful!" Lust radiated from his eyes. "What are you doing here?" he asked, kicking off his shoes.

"I miss you, baby. I couldn't go another day, so I figured I'd adjust my schedule and come see you before you go to sleep," I said, slowly and sensually rubbing on my breasts.

He couldn't get out of his clothes fast enough. The sight of my nakedness and me touching myself had his dick at full staff.

"However, I'm gonna need you to head that way," I said, pointing towards the bathroom. "Hit that water, then come hit this." I patted my pussy.

"That's how you gon' do me?"

I inserted two fingers inside my pussy, wiggled them, pulled them out and slowly sucked them as he watched. "Mmm... don't you wanna come taste all this?" I teased.

"Can I at least taste your fingers?"

I fingered myself again, then held them to his mouth. He licked and sucked my fingers so sensually it made my toes tingle.

"Gimme ten minutes, baby," he said, hurrying to the shower.

I laid on my stomach and flipped through the music channels. I needed something to set the mood. Carl returned with a towel wrapped around his waist. His muscular pecks and abs were a sight for sore eyes. "C'mere," I said, enticingly motioning with my finger.

He stopped in front of me. I removed the towel with one hand. His semi-hardness dangled before me. My mouth watered in anticipation of tasting it. I reached out and grabbed it. I kissed it. I licked up, down, and all around, then put it in my mouth. Within seconds, it was at full staff and hard as a baseball bat. I had plans for all this, so I deep throated it twice, then laid back on the bed so he could have his way with me.

He crawled onto the bed after me. He held my left foot up and kissed my toes, working his way toward my big toe. He sensually sucked on it as if he'd mistaken my red toenail polish to be a strawberry.

The moistness of his mouth, lips, and tongue sent tingling sensations racing up my leg and through my body as he licked up my inner thigh until he reached my lotus flower. His nose and lips brushed over my wet mound as he inhaled my essence. The initial contact of his tongue tracing my pussy lips felt extraordinarily good. He licked inside of me and began performing twists, turns, and odd configurations.

"Oh, Carl... ooooo, baby, I miss you," I moaned, putting my feet on his shoulders.

Like a thirsty puppy, he began lapping my clit. The sensation intensified, making my body tingle. An orgasm was building up. I caressed his bald head with both hands, vehemently moaning, "Baby, baby, baby, I'm cummin'... oooh!" My sweet nectar glistened all over his lips and ran down the crack of my ass.

He kissed up my fiending body until he hovered over me in a dominating position, reminding me of my femininity. He tried to tease me by rubbing the tip of his dick on my pussy, but I was having none of that. I moved his hand and guided it in myself. I gasped as it took my breath away.

"You just gon' take the dick, huh?" he laughed.

"It's mine, and I want it now."

Words alone can't describe the pleasure I felt as my walls expanded to accommodate the space his dick commanded. With one hand spreading my leg and the other braced against the headboard, he sucked on my nipples and vigorously thrusted in a circular motion, causing my head to bang against the headboard with each upstroke. I didn't care. It felt so damn good at that point I was willing to endure a concussion if need be.

"Yesss, daddy. Oooh, I love this dick!" I moaned aloud as my walls contracted in a pulsating manner. This was the orgasm my body craved.

Sensing I was about to erupt, Carl pushed both of my legs back until my toes latched onto the headboard, and then proceeded to pound incessantly. "Um-hmmm, this what you want, ain't it?" he panted, breathing heavily.

As the electrifying currents rippled throughout my body, my legs began to tremble uncontrollably. "Oh, my God... yes... yesss... babyyyy!" *SWOOSH!! SWOOSH!!* I screamed as my orgasm gushed forth like a tsunami.

He leaned back on his knees and watched as I lay drowning in ecstasy. After I stopped convulsing, I reached over on the nightstand, grabbed the deep throat spray, and then put a Listerine strip in my mouth.

"Stand up," I ordered.

"In the bed?" he asked, curious.

"Yeah."

He stood up, his head almost at the ceiling. I grabbed ahold of his massive dick and began teasing the swollen head in my mouth, gradually taking it in and out.

"Ooh, shit! What's this?" he asked as the tingly, cool sensation of the strip kicked in.

I responded by bobbing up and down, slurping back and forth, and swirling my tongue around the head.

"Get it, baby," he moaned in delight, rubbing the back of my neck.

He closed his eyes and had a tranquil expression on his face. Turned on by his obvious enjoyment, my clit pulsated and my mouth wettened. As he slowly face-fucked me, I massaged his balls and the area below them. I felt his scrotum swell and rise, so I knew he was close to exploding. I picked up the pace. I sucked and slurped profusely while stroking him.

"Damn, Michaela... I'm cummin'!" he groaned out loud.

I deep throated his dick. His legs slightly buckled as he looked down at me, shocked to see how much I was able to ingest. His dick began pulsating. He exploded down my throat. The force of the nut felt like it had been shot out of a cannon. I stared up at him. I was breathing through my nose to control my gag reflex, as instructed by the chick I reached out to.

Mesmerized, Carl watched me drain his dick until his legs were about to give out. When I pulled his dick out of my mouth, he collapsed on the bed, lifeless. Yesss! Shoutout to my *cream pie girls!*

Chapter 8

(Brooke)

Deciding to open my heart to loving another man, and to being loved, reinvigorated my spirit. For the first time in four years, I felt alive. I was turning the pitiful pages of my life to a new chapter, and I couldn't think of a better man than Seven to write my life with.

Over the course of three weeks, the level of intimacy we shared brought us closer and closer. We talked every day, sometimes for hours at a time, which was easy to do because he was well-versed and knowledgeable about many things. He made me laugh, challenged my intellect, and listened intently when I spoke.

We met for lunch several times a week. These meet-ups usually led to us going back to his place until it was time for me to pick up Yasmin. Sex was great. I was getting used to how big his dick was. But like Michaela testified, every time felt like it was the first time. Don't get me wrong, the sex was amazing, but it was his attention to the small things that blew my mind. His memory of the ways I liked to be touched, licked, and kissed was exceptional. He recognized the look I gave him when I wanted more, and he knew the angle and pace that made me climax faster and harder. Most guys don't spend enough time studying body language to pick up on those cues, but he did.

Seven understood I was in the process of rebuilding my self-esteem and openness, and he was very patient with me. He allowed me to move at the pace I was comfortable with. He encouraged me to be true to my nature no matter the situation or circumstance I faced.

Thursday's workout carried over our usual time, so I was running a little behind schedule for my lunch date with Seven. I had just got out the shower and was moisturizing my body when, unexpectedly, the doorbell rang. I grabbed my cell phone to see who it was by way of my security app.

"Can I help you?" I asked. My voice went through the doorbell's speaker.

"I have a delivery for a Ms. Brooke Collins," said a white, female courier.

"One second, please."

I hadn't ordered anything, so I wasn't expecting anything. I put on my robe and headed downstairs. When I opened the door, the woman was holding a crystal vase with beautiful flowers in it. In her other hand was a manilla envelope. I signed for them, then shut the door.

The flowers smelled fresh, like they had just been picked. I walked into the kitchen and sat the vase on the island counter, then opened the card attached to it.

Hope these Venus flowers brighten your day as thoughts of you have brightened mine, Queen!

I opened the envelope and pulled out a copy of the *Tavistock Institute: Human Relations* book. The memo sticker on it read: *Enjoy! Seven.*

The smile on my face was larger than a little girl whose face lights up when she sees her gifts under the Christmas tree on Christmas morning.

The time it took to sign for and open the gift wasn't long, but it did put me further behind. Elated, I ran upstairs and finished getting dressed. Immediately afterwards, I rushed out the door. It was time to go see my man.

As I pulled into Red Lobster's parking lot, I saw Seven's black Mercedes Benz truck parked in the row furthest from the door. I didn't blame him. The last thing I'd want is for someone to damage my $200,000 truck, too. I parked beside him.

I entered the restaurant and looked around. Seven held his hand up and waved me over to the window booth he was seated at.

"Hey, gorgeous," he said, sliding out to greet me.

"Sorry I'm so late," I replied with a hug and a kiss. "Thank you for those lovely flowers and the book! How, better yet, where did you find a copy?" I was shocked he was able to get one.

He looked around the restaurant as if we were being watched. "It's classified information, so if I tell you, I might have to kill you," he kidded. "Nah, I called in a favor with my folks out in California who owns a great bookstore."

"Well, thank you again. I got held up at the gym, and then the courier showed up and that threw me further behind," I smiled, "but I'm here now, and I'm excited to see you."

"It's all good, luv. I was sitting here on my phone, checking out some art from a guy in Seattle. He got some dope work." He showed me some of the pictures on his phone. "I wanna showcase some of his paintings at our next exhibit."

"When is the next exhibit?"

"I got a few more artists I wanna see work from first, but I'm thinking next month some time."

A dark-skinned lady with red hair came to take our order. I ordered chicken strips with the vegetable medley and a lemonade. Seven ordered the fish and chips with an iced tea. The waitress collected our menus and left.

"Speaking of next month, my girl Michaela is planning a couples trip to Jamaica for her boyfriend's birthday, and I was hopiiing," I said, dragging it out as I gave him a sexy stare, "... you would like to accompany me."

"You just gon' bat them pretty eyes at me like that to persuade me, huh?" he said with a heartful laugh.

"Aye, I'm trying to make it happen."

"One thing is for certain, all you gotta do is say the word and I'm pulling up on you. Besides, I can use a vacation myself. How much is the trip?"

"It's on me!" I answered, smiling, happy to show love to my man.

As we enjoyed our food, we engaged in general conversation, occasionally sharing a few laughs. He liked making fun of my facial expressions during sex. Funny thing is, every time he spoke, I stared at his supple lips, envisioning them kissing all over my body in Jamaica.

"I got something I'd like to ask you."

"Go ahead," I said.

"If you don't have plans Saturday, I'd love to take you and Yasmin on a date. There's going to be a carnival over by the stadium I'd like to take y'all to."

His request to take *us* on a date was flattering, and it turned me on. The thought of introducing him to Yasmin at the carnival seemed like a good idea.

"We'd love to go on a date with you this Saturday," I said smiling.

I checked my watch and saw I had an hour and a half before it was time to go get Yasmin. He paid for lunch, and we went back to his place for a little afternoon fun.

Never in a million years could I have thought my life would change the way it had, as fast as it had. A month before, I was a prisoner to my own heart. I was lonely and sexually frustrated. But after meeting Seven, I felt free, adventurous, and had more sex than the previous four years combined.

After putting Yasmin down for the night, I poured a glass of wine and nestled up in the corner of the sofa with my new book, excited to finally read it. I dozed off minutes into the first chapter.

When Saturday morning came, I got up and went downstairs to make coffee and get my day started. The floral scent of the beautiful flowers filled the house with positive energy. While waiting on the expresso machine to work its magic, I sat on the island stool and thought about *our* date with Seven. I was curious to see how Yasmin would react to being around a man other than her father. I wondered if Seven would interact with a child that belonged to another man. And then there was the mystery of how I would and should act with both.

Once the coffee was ready, I poured some into my porcelain mug. My thoughts quickly shifted to what Seven and I could do to make our trip to Jamaica all the more special. The fashionista in me began plotting what outfits, swimsuits, dresses, and lingerie to bring. Just thinking about it made me excited.

It was a typical summer day in Georgia – sunny, hot, humid. Because of the heat index, Seven said he'd pick us up at 6:30pm. This gave it time to cool down.

Like every other Saturday morning, I put on some relaxing music, cleaned the house, changed the bedding, washed a few loads of clothes, then braided Yasmin's hair, decorating the ends with her favorite, color beads – pink and purple. Knowing we would be doing a lot of walking, I dressed her in a cute, short outfit that matched her multi-colored Nike Air Max shoes. I put on white hot-shorts, a blue tank-top, and white Huarache sneakers. I was pleased when I checked myself in the mirror; I liked how tone my legs and butt looked… courtesy of the squats and lunges from the day before, of course.

At 6:30pm, Seven's black Mercedes Benz truck was in my driveway. He put Yasmin's car seat in for me while I activated the house alarm and locked up. I finished and went to strap Yasmin in.

"Yas, this is Seven. Say hi."

"Hi," she said with her light voice.

"Hi, princess. It's nice to finally meet you." Seven flashed a charming smile and turned to me. "She's beautiful, Brooke. Got her mother's sexy eyes."

"Thank you."

After I sat down and secured my seatbelt, I leaned over and kissed Seven. "You look nice, handsome," I complimented, checking him out. He was dressed in a tan, two-piece, linen short set; chocolate, suede Ferragamo driving loafers; and his locs were freshly braided to the back.

"So do you, beautiful. You ready to have some fun?" he asked while looking back at Yas.

"Ready!" she shouted enthusiastically.

I was shocked by her reaction. *So far, so good.*

We parked two blocks away from the carnival. I was a little concerned because I didn't bring my stroller, but Seven assured me everything would be okay. He hoisted her up around his neck, which she loved because of the view. When we reached the gate, Seven paid our admission with Yasmin still on his shoulders. We then entered the grounds.

The smell of cotton candy, corn dogs, and funnel cakes wafted in the air as crowds of people moved to and fro. The ringing of bells and flashing of lights lured people to try their hands at one game or another. Seven held my hand and led us through the traffic, stopping in front of the cotton candy stand.

"You want some cotton candy, Yasmin?"

Yas had never been to a carnival or eaten cotton candy before.

"Yes," she happily replied.

"What color you want, Yas? Pink or blue?" I asked.

"Pink!" she shouted excitedly.

We watched as the attendant worked the spindle and made our stick. He handed it to Yasmin and then turned to Seven to get paid.

The three of us picked at the cotton candy as we made our way over to the kid-friendly rides. First up were the teacups that spin around. I thought Yas would be a little timid, if not scared, to do anything; however, she turned out to be fearless. She wanted to ride every ride multiple times, especially the merry-go-round. She loved sitting on the horses.

Watching Yas smile and laugh as she interacted with Seven was a beautiful sight. She was having a good time, and so was I. Within an hour, Seven had become her new, best friend.

We decided to take a break from the rides and go grab a bite to eat. We settled on the corndog stand. After getting our order, we sat on a nearby bench.

Seven took a bite of his corndog and reminisced. "I used to love these when I was a kid."

"I know, right? I haven't been to a carnival in years," I stated then bit into my corndog.

"Whaaat!" Seven seemed to be genuinely surprised.

"Honest to God truth."

He smiled. "I rolled past here the other day when they were setting up and instantly thought about y'all."

"Well, I'm glad you did," I said, blushing. Not wanting it to be so obvious, I quickly changed the conversation. "Are you sure you don't have any kids, 'cause you sure do have a way with her?"

"Nah, no kids. I love kids and kids love me. Kids are honest. Their divine instincts haven't been deprogrammed yet, so they feed off a individual's energy. If it's positive, they'll receive you. If it's negative, they'll cry, kick, and scream to get away from you every time you come around'em."

His assessment was spot-on. "Do you want children?"

"Oh, absolutely!" he answered emphatically. "I'd like to have a big family one day."

"How big is big?" I asked inquisitively.

"'Bout eight or nine kids," he said jokingly.

"Oooh, you tried it!" I laughed, stunned by the outrageous number.

"Seriously, tho... two or four kids would be nice." He took the last bite of his corndog.

Those numbers are reasonable... and doable.

"What about you?" asked Seven. "Do you want more kids?"

"I do. It would be nice for Yas to have a sibling or two to grow up with."

After Seven scarfed down his second corndog, we decided to get some snow cones. We walked around, letting Yas enjoy herself. We had so much fun. Seven played the sledgehammer strength test and made the puck go up and hit the bell. He let Yasmin pick out the overstuffed animal she wanted. She chose the pink unicorn, of course.

As the sun slowly faded, so did the family-oriented crowd. More and more unsupervised teenagers began roaming around. Having watched me and Seven hold hands all day, Yas latched onto his other hand as we made our way to the front. Out of nowhere, someone called my name. *Brooke!* I turned around and saw Hanifa, Jahsani, and the twins.

"Hey, Nifa!" I said, happy to see her.

Seven greeted Jahsani, "Peace, king."

"Peace."

Hanifa smiled at Seven and I's open display of affection. I blushed at her nonverbal acknowledgement.

"You go, girl!" she teased me. Looking at Yas, she asked, "Did you have fun, Yas?"

"Yes. I got on the horses and look what I got." She pointed to the unicorn I carried.

"That's pretty, Yas!" replied Hanifa, who then looked at me. "How long y'all been here?"

"Long enough!" I answered, ready to go. "Girl, she done wore me out. We're on our way out. What about y'all?"

"We just got here about twenty minutes ago. You know he don't close the shop til seven."

"Aight. Well, y'all have fun and be safe."

"Bye, Yas!" said Hanifa.

"Bye-bye."

The smooth sounds of Blackstreet's *Before I let You Go* played as we cruised down the freeway. I looked back to check on Yas; she was knocked out. A sense of peace and joy came over me that very instance. This was what I had been yearning for for years – someone to hold hands with, to do things with, to learn from, and to feel appreciated by. It was obvious that the more time I spent around Seven, the deeper in love I'd fall.

Seven parked in the driveway and offered to carry Yasmin inside in her car seat for me. The sconce hanging on the wall in the foyer was the only light when we entered the house. I walked towards the kitchen and cut the lights on so I could key in the code to disarm the alarm while he sat the car seat on the sofa.

"You have a lovely home, Brooke," he said, looking around.

"Thank you. Would you like something to drink? I don't have any of that stuff you have, but I have wine," I offered.

"Wine would be perfect."

"Okay. Let me get her situated and I'll be right back."

I took Yas out of her car seat and carried her up to her room. I undressed her, tucked her into bed, then returned downstairs. I poured two glasses of wine and joined Seven on the sofa.

"You oughta be ashamed of yourself. Got my baby up there passed out like that," I joked while taking off my sneakers.

"I'll gladly do it every day if given the chance," he smiled.

"I bet you would. She's already spoiled, and the last thing I need is for you to compound that."

"What's wrong with that? She deserves to be spoiled, and so do you, queen." He signaled for me to put my feet in his lap. "Give'em to me."

I melted as he rubbed my arches with his thumbs. "Aaah! That feels so good," I exhaled and took a sip of wine.

"Can I do that for you?"

I was unsure what he meant. "Do what for me?"

"Spoil y'all."

My lingering insecurities came to the surface. "Seven, I'm not the type of woman who's into you because of the things you can buy me. I'm into you because you're a beautiful soul. You don't have to spoil us."

He burst out laughing. "What does any of what you said have to do with me spoiling y'all. I didn't mention a thing about 'buy things.'"

"Well, what do you mean?"

"Brooke, you're a phenomenal woman and mother. You have a beautiful daughter, and both of y'all are worthy of the best a man can give y'all. When I say spoil y'all, I'm referring to showering y'all with affection, time, energy, and love. Whatever it takes to put a smile on y'all face. Keep in mind, how you receive love will define her reality of what love is."

His response gave me a mental orgasm. It was everything I ever wanted, and it was what I wanted for Yas. "I apologize." I paused briefly before speaking again. "Seven, you're everything I ever wanted in a man. Unfortunately, I'm still adjusting to being treated with such admiration and affection. Today alone was better than the last four years I spent with him." I paused again. My emotions had caused my voice to crack. "I can't begin to tell you how special I felt when you held my hand, then Yas grabbed your other hand." A tear rolled down my face.

"It's all good, beautiful. You don't ever have to worry about feeling like you're not important to me, you hear me?"

I nodded my head while he wiped away my tears.

"Now back to my question. Can I spoil y'all?"

"Yes, baby," I answered in a feeble tone.

"C'mere, baby," he said, motioning for me.

I sat my glass on the coffee table, then straddled his lap. We sat there holding each other without saying a word. His embrace was firm, warm, and comforting. His cologne was intoxicating. It sent my hormones into overdrive. I kissed his soft lips twice. Our tongues then began going back and forth as he caressed my butt. I panted with wantonness. I could feel his nature rising in the thin material he wore. It was getting harder by the second.

I'd never considered a set day or time for him to be able to come to my house or spend the night. After the amazing day we shared, however, this night was going to be a groundbreaking moment in our relationship. I stood up, took him by the hand, and led him upstairs to my bedroom.

It was dark with just a glimmer of lunar light peeking through a crack in the curtains. We resumed kissing and began undressing one another. I was in control and planned on catering to him like the king he is. I pushed him onto the bed and positioned myself on his left side so he could watch as I kissed and licked up and down his long shaft. Taking my time, I sucked in and out until it was soaked. I then licked his balls. I sucked one after the other while slowly stroking his dick. "Aaah... that feels amazing, baby," he uttered in delight.

I licked my way back up to the head and started bobbing, simultaneously slurping, smacking, moaning, and twisting my grip as I stroked it. "Work it, Brooke!" he moaned. He reached behind me and began playing with my pussy. I was soaking wet.

I straddled his lap and guided it in, trying to prepare for the initial shock, but it still made me gasp. "Uuuaah!" After a few minutes, I began rocking back and forth, causing his dick to massage my clit, which sent my moans to a vociferous frenzy. "Oh, Seven... oh, Seven... oooh, yo' dick so big!"

I leaned back with my hips and began impaling myself. I bounced up and down like I was a jockey riding a horse at the Kentucky Derby. His hands gripped my butt, forcing me to go faster and harder. With each thrust, it felt like he was pushing up into my stomach. I felt an electrifying sensation building.

We were both being loud and panting heavily. His huge, hard dick had me hitting high notes like Minnie Rippleton. My tight, creamy pussy had him making sex faces, hissing like a snake. "Aaah, sh-sh-shit, Brooke! Sh-shit, I'm cummin', baby... s-sh-get it, baby." The more he struggled to get his words out, the more forcefully he fucked. The increase in pace and pressure made me scream aloud as my orgasm exploded like a super nova. I hissed, "S-Seven... S-S-Seven... yesss, yesss... yesss!" I stammered.

Then out of nowhere, I heard, "Mommy. You okay, mommy?" the sound of Yasmin's faint voice scared the shit out of me. She stood right by the side of the bed rubbing her eyes. Torn between ecstasy and shame, I tried to steady my breathing and act calm.

"I'm... I'm okay, baby. Go back to your room and get in the bed," I said, feeling out of breath. Seven's pulsating dick inside of me didn't help. He laid there silently without so much as a breath of air coming from him.

"I wanna sleep with you, mommy," whined Yas.

Thank God it was dark in the room, or else she would have seen more than the silhouette of my body. I slowly dismounted Seven. His dick flailed about like a recoiled spring. I put my robe on and carried Yasmin back to her room and laid with her until she dozed back off.

Seven was laying awake in the bed when I returned. Embarrassed beyond words, I took off my robe and got into bed. I laid my head on his chest.

"You aight?" he asked.

I shook my head as I tried to process what had just happened. "I can't believe what just happened," I stated. I'm a terrible mother. I should've closed my door. I was too loud," I ranted.

"Brooke, stop. Breathe," he instructed, trying to calm me down. "You're not a terrible mother. She didn't see anything, so she'll be okay."

"How can you say that? I don't even know how long she was standing there, Seven," I said panicky.

"Listen to me, Brooke. She'll be fine. She'll wake up tomorrow like nothing ever happened. Trust me."

Despite his kind words and assurances, the lingering scent of sex in the air didn't make me feel better about myself.

"Would you like for me to leave?"

The last thing I needed was to be alone with my guilty conscience. "No. Please stay with me."

He consoled me as I laid on his chest and fell asleep.

It was 9am and Yas still hadn't got up. Seven was still asleep, so I quietly slipped out of bed, put my robe on, and went to check on her. She was knocked out.

Seven's eyes opened as I got back into bed. Yawning, he greeted me in his usual fashion. "Good morning, beautiful."

"Good morning," I replied, then kissed him. "How did you sleep?"

"Like a baby. Whenever I'm with you, everything in my world is perfect," he said, rubbing my thigh.

His comment made me blush. Truth be told, I felt the same way about him. "Okay, don't start nothing this morning. You already got me busted last night," I said, laughing.

"I got you busted? I guess yo' opera-like performance didn't have anything to do with it, huh?" he asked, then began mimicking the way I moaned and yelled out.

"Shut up!" I laughed. "Aye, I couldn't help it."

"It's cool. I accept part of the blame, baby."

Waking up to his warm body, big smile, and laughter felt good. "Can you stay for breakfast?" I asked.

"Absolutely."

I got up and put on my green spandex shorts and a t-shirt and went downstairs to get started on our meal. It was only a few minutes later when Yas woke up and came down.

"Hey, mommy's angel. You want some apple juice?"

"Yes."

Seven came down the stairs just as I was flipping over the last omelet. Yasmin's eyes lit up with excitement.

"We going to get on the horses again?" she asked him.

I jumped in before he had time to say yes. "Not today, Yas. Seven gotta go to work. Maybe next time."

She looked skeptically at him. "You gotta go to work?"

"Yeah. We'll go another time, princess."

I plated the turkey bacon and omelet, then joined them at the table. Yas asked Seven a thousand questions as we ate. Unsurprisingly, he patiently answered every one of them. I expected her to ask about last night, but she never did.

I cleaned the kitchen after we finished eating. While I was doing so, Yas showed Seven every doll she had in the play area. I was enjoying the vibe, but I knew it had to end.

"Well, luv, I'mma get going. Thanks for breakfast and an amazing night."

"Thank you for the lovely date and for staying with me last night." I hugged and kissed him.

The doorbell unexpectedly rang. Seven was saying his goodbyes to Yas as I made my way to the door. I opened the door and saw Darius standing there looking at Seven's truck. Instantly, my heart dropped into my stomach. It wasn't his weekend to get

Yasmin, so I didn't understand why he was at my door, especially without calling first.

"Can I come in?" he calmly asked.

"Sure." I stepped aside.

It was a terribly awkward moment, as Seven was on his way to the door.

"Seven, this is Yasmin's father, Darius. Darius, this is Seven."

The look on Darius's face was stoic.

"Peace, king," said Seven.

"What's up," replied Darius.

"Daddy!" shouted Yasmin, running and jumping into Darius's arms.

"Hey, baby!"

Seven gave me a hug, then left.

I closed the door and walked back to the kitchen to get a glass of water. Darius followed me.

"What's going on?" he asked.

"What you mean 'what's going on?'"

"I've been calling your phone all morning, but it keeps going to voicemail, so I came to check on y'all."

"My battery probably dead. We good, tho," I said, then took a sip of water.

"That's yo' new man with the G650?" he asked sarcastically.

"Don't do that."

"Do what? I simply asked if that's the guy you've been going out with. He's around my daughter and in my house. I should be able to know who he is."

He put Yasmin down. She went into the family room with her toys.

"First off, this is no longer your house. It's my house. And if you must know, that's who I've been dating. You checked on us and can see we're fine, so is there anything else?"

The sight of flowers made him pause. He sat on one of the island stools. "Look, Brooke, I know things between us the past few years haven't been the best... primarily, on my end. The lawyer called the other day about finalizing the divorce, but I think we should give it another try. I still love you and wanna make our family whole again."

The nerve of him. First, he tries to come up in here like he checkin' me, and now he wants to give us another try. Boy, bye. "Darius, you're Yasmin's father and I will always love you, but I'm no longer in love with you. I've waited four years for you to do right by me, love me, and appreciate me, but you didn't. I've finally found myself again. I'm happy and in love with Seven. He's good to us, and he's the reason I have peace and joy in my heart again. You and I work well together as parents, just not well together as a couple. I've accepted that we've outgrown each other and our marriage. I don't hold any ill feelings toward you; in fact, I hope you find someone who can make you happy, because I couldn't."

He sat there silently staring at my calm demeanor, processing every word I expressed. Once it settled in, he took a deep breath, then got up and quietly walked out. The door closing brought closure to our marriage, and it set me emotionally free.

Chapter 9

(Hanifa)

Thank goodness the uncomfortableness of cramping was beginning to subside. Because of my healthy diet, my cycle only lasted four days. Luckily, I had Jahsani. He understood this was a very sensitive and hormonal time for me, so he cooked, cleaned, and took the kids out the house so I could rest or just have some peace and quiet.

My Sunday morning was just getting started. I made a cup of Burdock tea to help with feeling bloated, then went into the backyard to check on the garden. After finishing my tea, I grabbed the water hose and watered the soil while performing libations to the ancestors. I then went and laid back down.

Jahsani and the kids cooked and brought me breakfast in bed. This was our family weekend. We went to the carnival yesterday. Jahsani planned on cranking up the grill today. All I was going to do was make my fruity beans (baked beans with brown sugar and pineapples) and potato salad. I didn't like the way he made his. He made his like his mother made hers – runny and bland.

Around 1pm, I got up and took a shower, then put on some comfortable shorts to lounge around in. Jahlissa and I were in the kitchen cutting up potatoes when Jahsani came downstairs with my phone in his hand. "Brooke's on the phone," he said, handing it to me.

"Hello?"

"Girl, are you busy?" she asked in a deadened tone.

"Not really. What's going on?" I was concerned.

"You ain't gon' believe this shit!"

Judging by the tone of her voice, whatever it was, it was serious. I wiped my hands off on the towel and stepped outside on the patio for some privacy.

"What happened, Brooke?"

"Where should I begin?" She took a deep breath. "Girl, I need a pow-wow and a drink to calm my nerves."

"I'm here. Grab a bottle and pull up."

"Aight. See you in a minute."

"Peace."

Jahsani was helping Jahlissa when I went back into the kitchen.

"Un-un, stop. Don't be trying to sabotage my potato salad," I barked, running him off.

"Is everything aight with Brooke?" he asked.

"I hope so. She on her way over here, so would you mind taking them to the store with you when she get here?"

"No problem, baby."

Jahlissa and I finished getting the side dishes ready. I put the baked beans in the oven while she put the potato salad in the refrigerator. Teaching her how to cook was our little right of passage, just as it was mine with my mother and grandmother. I'm still working on getting her interested in gardening. Funny thing is, Jahlil likes working in the garden with me. Go figure.

Brooke showed up at 2pm with a confounded look on her face. Jahsani had the grill ready for when he returned from the store. When he walked in the kitchen and saw Brooke, he greeted her as he always did.

"Aye, what up, sis?" He gave her a friendly hug.

"Nothing much. What's up with you?"

"'Bout to run to the market and get some fresh salmon, wings, and burgers so I can do my thing on the grill."

"That sounds good. Let me give you a couple of dollars to get some boneless chicken breasts to throw on there for me and Yas."

"That's cool. 'Nifa, you need me to pick up anything else while I'm out?"

"Nah, I'm good, baby."

"Aight. Be back in a minute." He kissed me, got $20 from Brooke, then left out.

Brooke poured us a glass of wine while I went to get the joint I had rolled earlier. When I returned, we went outside and sat at the table on the patio and fired it up.

"What's going on, girl?" I asked.

"Peep this shit. When you saw us yesterday, Seven was taking me and Yas on a date. At first I was hesitant because I've never had another man around her, but she took to him like she's known him her whole life."

I passed the joint to her. "I saw y'all holdinhg hands, looking like the Huckstables with locs," I kidded. "Y'all look cute together, and you looked happy."

"The two of them had a ball together!" She hit the joint and passed it back. "So, Yas was knocked out when we got home, so I invited him in to chill for a minute. One thing led to another, and I took him upstairs to my room." She paused to take a sip of wine. I passed the joint back and listened with an attentive ear. "Girrrl, we getting it in! I'm riding him like I'm Broke Back Mountain, breathing heavy, moaning loud, and talking shit. Why soon as we both explode, Yas walk in and call my name; she was standing right next to the bed." She was shaking her head.

My mouth like to hit the ground. "You lying!" I replied, shocked.

She passed the joint back. "'Nifa, I've never felt so ashamed of myself."

The look on her face was pure shame. "How long had she been there?"

"I don't know."

"Do you think she saw anything?"

"I don't think so. It was pitch black in the room. Thank God I didn't have the bathroom light on."

"You didn't close the door?" I asked perplexed.

"Girl, I haven't had sex in that house in two years. I forgot to close it."

I took a sip of wine, took the last hit of the joint, then put it out. My high kick in and Brooke was starting to mellow out.

"What was Seven doing during all of this?"

"Laying there like he was invisible." We both laughed.

"Y'all done traumatized my niecey-poo!"

"But wait, there's more," she said.

"More? Damn!"

We both took a sip of wine.

"So, Seven spent the night because I didn't wanna be alone with that on my mind. I made breakfast this morning, and you already know Yas talked his head off," she couldn't help from laughing. "Then, as he was leaving, the doorbell rings. I open it. It's Darius."

"You lying!"

"On Yas I'm not," she said, raising her right hand like she was being sworn in to testify. "Can you say awkward?!? I introduced Darius as Yas's father, then Seven to Darius."

"What Darius say?" I asked, being petty.

"He had a blank look on his face. They were cordial. Seven left, then I went in the kitchen to get some water because my mouth was dry." She paused to finish her last bit of wine. "Pour me another one. I've had a helluva weekend."

I poured us another glass of wine and patiently waited for the rest of the story.

"Do you know this fool talking 'bout I got people around his daughter he don't know, and in his house," she griped while mimicking Darius's voice.

"Quit playing."

"Girl, I shut that shit down ASAP! That's my house! And I can have whoever I want up in there whenever I feel good and ready."

"He trippin'. He just mad you moved on, so he trying to control you."

"Wait, here go the funny part. He said he don't think we should get a divorce, that we should give us another try for the sake of our family." The look of disbelief on her face was poignant. "You keep trying when you fall off a bike or fail a test, but when someone shit on you, disrespect you, and treat you like shit for years, you move on!"

"That part!" I agreed with her.

"I looked him dead in the eye and told him I'm in love with Seven, I'm happy, I feel better mentally and spiritually than ever before, and that we've outgrown each other and the marriage. I wished him well and said I hope he finds someone to make him happy since I couldn't."

"Ooh, go girl! I could only imagine the sick look on his face when you told him you're in love with Seven, and happy." "He didn't say anything. He just got up and left."

All I could do was shake my head in disbelief. "Brooke, you're a reality show waiting to happen... Love and Education Atlanta!" We both started laughing.

Jahsani and the kids returned. He went ahead and got started on the grill as we sat at the table talking and watching him do his thing. I tried not to make fun of Brooke's situation, but too many puns came to mind.

"Y'all coming to Jamaica for Carl's birthday, right?"

"You already know!" I said, smiling. "We're overdue for a vacation without the kids."

Jahsani turned around with the tongs in hand. "Is Seven coming with you?" he asked Brooke.

Her face lit up like the red light on the Krispy Kreme sign. "He is," she answered, blushing.

"I'm so happy for you, Brooke. Ever since y'all been kicking it, you're always smiling, giddy, and full of life. Then again, when you getting that Mandingo on a regular, any woman would be happier," I said, teasing her.

"Whatever!" she said, laughing. "I can't wait to put my feet in the ocean, lay out in the sun, and just relax because, before you know it, the school year will be here."

"I can't wait either, so these kids can get on somebody else's nerves beside mine." I laughed and took a sip of wine. "What you taking with you on the trip?"

"I don't know yet. I know I'm going to the mall this week to see what catches my eye. What about you?"

"No clue. I know Michaela mentioned she wanted everyone to wear all white to her birthday dinner, so I gotta find something cute to wear for that."

Jahsani finished grilling. Brooke fixed her and Yasmin some plates and then left.

Me, Jahsani, and the kids ate on the patio and enjoyed the rest of the day together. We played a few games of Uno until Jahsani started cheating to help Jahlissa win. She's such a daddy's girl. No matter what we played, she always wanted to be on his team. Jahlil and I didn't mind because our duo was usually the winning team.

Moments like these with the kids were sacred to me. Showing them what family and black excellence is has always been important to me. I wanted them to grow up knowing what love looks and feels like.

As nightfall settled in, the kids drifted to their separate spaces in the house. Jahsani and I relaxed on the patio, snuggled up on the love seat with a bottle of wine.

"Thanks for everything this weekend, baby. I truly appreciate it," I said to him.

"It's all good, queen. You know whatever-however this family needs me, I'll step up." He kissed me on my forehead.

"Can you believe we're coming up on ten years already?"

"Yo, it seems like only yesterday I walked into the Waffle House and saw you coming out the restroom with tissue stuck to the bottom of your shoe. I couldn't let you go by without saying something to you," he said with a hearty laugh.

"I'm glad you did. If you would've told me then that ten years later we'd be married, have twins, a nice house, and our own businesses, I wouldn't have believed you."

"I knew on our first date I was going to marry you."

"Quit lying," I said, facing him. "You was just trying to get some... wit' yo' nasty self."

"True. But I knew there was something special about you. You were conscious, comfortable in your own skin, and your energy was warm and inviting." He took a drink of wine. "When did you realize I was the one for you, baby?"

That was easy to answer because it was a day I would always remember.

"On our third date when you took me to the SWV and Monica concert. When we got back to your apartment, you played Michel'le's *Something in My Heart* while we chilled on the couch. You told me you love me, and that no matter what, in this lifetime or the next, your spirit wouldn't have peace until we were together. I thought that was so beautiful. That night was when we first made love."

He laughed. "Yeah, I remember that night. Michel'le was my fa sho panty dropper song. We've come a long way in a short period of time, baby. One thing I got right in this life is falling in love with you. Hanifa, you are my world, my best friend, and the best wife any man could hope for. You're an excellent mother, smart businesswoman, and a beloved friend by all who know you. You have enriched my life in so many ways, and I just want you to know I adore the ground you walk on, baby," he sincerely stated.

Tears streaked down my face. I loved how Jahsani wasn't afraid to share his feelings with me, or to be seen emotionally vulnerable. He was strong, humble, aggressive when need be, but ever so gentle and loving.

Although I was crying, I was happy. Happy because – come this time next week – we would be in Jamaica, and I wouldn't have to worry about the *reds* ruining our fun.

Chapter 10

(Michaela)

The past two weeks had been mentally and emotionally exhausting. I made sure all balances for the trip were paid, flights booked, and reservations for the beach dinner reserved. All that was left to do was finish up my last two consultant obligations.

Most of the data I researched showed similar trends, despite them being different ventures. The most notable was the lack of access to capital to scale production so the business could meet demand. Based off the numbers and prior experiences, my ideas to combat the challenges both businesses faced were pragmatic.

Carl and I had toured several houses, but only one came close to meeting all of our must-haves. The house was in the Swanky section of East Atlanta. It was 2400 square feet with a detached, two-car garage and four bedrooms, one of which I could convert into my office. A nice open-floor plan, a finished basement for Carl, and a nice-sized backyard. The only issue was the price; it was listed at $20,000 over our approved loan amount. After growing tired of the house hunt, we discussed me paying the overage. I then called and asked our realtor to put in an offer for $410,000.

With the trip coming up on Friday, I decided Brooke and I would take the week off so our bodies could rest. Of course, she didn't protest one bit. Instead, as a token of appreciation for training her, Brooke offered to treat me to a half-hour session at

Lotus Steaming Spa. Free coochie pampering? I couldn't accept her offer fast enough.

We entered Lotus around noon. Tori was working the front desk. Brooke felt like having a little fun. With a wink of the eye, she said to Tori in a boisterous, disgruntled voice, "I wanna speak to the owner of this establishment!" Within two seconds, Hanifa emerged from the back to see what all the commotion was about. The look on her face was priceless.

Relieved at seeing our faces, Hanifa laughed and said, "I should've known it was Thelma and Louise. What y'all up to?"

Brooke spoke in her intellectual voice. "We've come to have our vaginas refreshed by the hot steam of your loveliest porter potties!"

All four of us burst out laughing.

"You stupid, Brooke," said Hanifa. "For real, shouldn't you two be at the gym or something?"

"Nope. Michaela gave us the week off, so I said, 'Let's go to Lotus, my treat.'"

Hanifa didn't waste any time countering Brooke's shenanigans with a ratchet retort of her own. "Well, ain't that something. Broke Back Mountain and Ol' Chattahoochie Coochie came to get their boxes refreshed before the trip so them boys can put their big mule legs inside them!" We laughed so hard we had tears in our eyes, especially Tori. Hanifa then got down to business. "Aight, c'mon back and let's get you ladies together."

She opened the door and led us to the back. Once there, she handed us a towel and a gown to put on. "Brooke, do you prefer music, 432 Htz meditation sounds, stones, or crystals?"

"I brought a crystal to meditate with, so the meditation sounds, please."

"Good. You need to clear your energy," teased Hanifa. "What about you, Michaela?"

"Let me get an amethyst crystal and the 432 Htz sounds, too, please."

"It'll be in your room. Enjoy, ladies!"

I sat on the throne and began my meditation by focusing on my breathing. Focusing on the breath allows the kundalini energy to rise up the spine. I exhaled internally and visualized my body pushing the negative energy out of my vagina. As the steam from the herbs rose, I felt the impurities within me being purged.

Thirty minutes later, my meditation was interrupted by the beeping noise of the timer going off. My vagina felt relaxed, moist, and rejuvenated. Personally, I felt spiritually reinvigorated, physically recharged, and mentally alert. I put my clothes back on and went back up front. Brooke and Hanifa were standing in the sitting area talking.

"What y'all about to get into?" asked Hanifa.

"Probably run over to Phipps Mall. I need to get a new swimsuit for all this juicy ass, and a few other things, too," I answered being silly.

"Well, hold on," said Hanifa, "I need to get a few things myself. Let me grab my purse and I'll follow y'all." She grabbed her purse from the back and quickly returned. Looking at Tori, she said, "Tori, I'm going to lunch. I should be back in an hour. Call me if you need anything."

"Okay. Bye, ladies. Have fun!"

Our cab pulled up to the drop off area in front of the airport at 6am. Carl checked our bags in while I paid the driver. Carmen and Will exited the cab behind us. She greeted me cheerfully while Will checked in their bags.

"Good morning!"

"Hey, girl! Your hair is cute," I said, complimenting her pixie cut with flip-dyed honey blonde. "You look like you ready to have a good time."

"I am. Soon as we touch down, I'm getting lit!"

After clearing the security area, we made our way through the airport to gate 23. Brooke and Seven were sitting together.

"Good morning, good morning!" I excitedly greeted them.

They both responded, "Good morning," in like fashion.

"Have you heard from Hanifa?"

"They're at the gift shop buying gum," Brooke answered while pointing at her and Jahsani.

Once we were all together, I introduced the guys to Will. Brooke and Hanifa were already familiar with Carmen since our days as dormmates in college. While waiting on the flight, I decided to let everyone know what was going on.

"Here's the deal, y'all. Everything at the resort has been taken care of in case you wanna do something. You can jet ski, go snorkeling, paddle boarding, hang out at the pools, in the sports bar, shoot pool, go scuba diving, zip lining, and/or get massages on the beach.

"Every bungalow is stocked with premium liquor. All drinks are free at any of the resort's bars, and all tips and gratuities have been taken care of." I paused to let them think it over. "If anyone wants to hang out tonight, they got live entertainment. Tomorrow night is my baby's birthday, and I'm asking everyone to wear white for dinner. Sunday is our last day on the island, so everyone can do their own thing if you like, but be careful because the flight leaves at 7am, and the driver will pick us up at 5:30. Any questions?"

There were no questions.

Carl wasn't fond of flying, so I took the window seat when we boarded. I figured he wouldn't think negative thoughts as long as we were talking. Between us talking freaky and me covertly fondling him, the only thing on his mind was getting to the island so he could get this WAP!

Two hours into the flight, the pilot announced we were in Jamaican airspace. The aerial views of clear, blue waters, white sand beaches, extravagant villas and resorts surrounded by a lush rainforest made me excited as the plane began its descent.

Everyone retrieved their bags. Wide-eyed, we made our way outside.

The weather was beautiful. It was sunny, warm, and not a cloud in the sky. A tall, dark-skinned man dressed in black slacks and a white shirt stood in front of a Sprinter van. He held up a placard with the name Jackson on it. I walked over to him.

"Good morning. I'm Michaela Jackson."

His eyes lit up with infatuation. He spoke with a sexy island accent. "Good morning. Welcome to Jamaica. My name is Winston, and I'll be your driver." He smiled the entire time he spoke. After introducing himself, he loaded our bags into the van.

Looks of excitement flooded everyone's eyes as we boarded the van and sat with our partners. Seeing my girl Brooke boo'ed up and happy was a beautiful thing considering all she'd been through the past four years. Winston pulled off at 11:30pm. I turned around in my seat to see what everyone was thinking.

"So, what y'all wanna do when we reach the resort?"

Jahsani quickly responded. "Get something to eat! I'm starvin'."

The consensus was unanimous.

"Aight. After we check in and get settled, let's meet up and go eat together."

Everyone agreed.

"Brooke, what y'all thinking about doing first?" asked Hanifa.

Brooke shrugged her shoulders. "I don't know. Jet skiing, maybe." She looked at Seven for confirmation.

"I'm wit' whatever you wanna do, baby."

Carmen was sold on the idea. "I'm definitely down with getting on the jet skis!" she enthusiastically stated.

Hanifa was shocked by Carmen's reaction. "You not scared of being on it out in the middle of the ocean?"

"Nope!"

"Girl," I said to Hanifa, "Carmen ride motorcycles. She can handle a jet ski."

My comment caught Seven's attention. "What kind of bike you got, Carmen?"

"A 2014, candy red and chrome Harley Davidson Bagger with a 30" front wheel. You ride?"

"Yeah. I got a Hayabusa."

"That's what's up. Will got one of those, too."

Carl also wanted to go jet skiing, so we agreed to meet up after we ate to go out on the water.

Jahsani called out to the driver, "Bredren, where are the spots the people from the island kick it at?"

Winston looked at us from the rearview mirror. "Depends on what ya lookin' for."

"We wanna kick it with the masses, feel the vibes, hear the dialect and candor, you know, take in the culture of the yard!"

Winston smiled. "Irie, bredren! To get a feel for the people, you gotta head into the hills of Blue Mountain. That's where the secluded waterfalls and lagoons are, and people playin' in the streams and chillin'. When you wanna hang out, hit Floyd's Pelican Bar. Good vibes and people there, but you can only get there by boat. For authentic Jamaican food, try Claudia's or Sonny's."

Everyone seemed interested in experiencing the true culture of Jamaica.

"Would it be possible for you to take us to some of those places?" I asked.

"Sure. Just let me know when y'all wanna go," Winston replied.

I turned back around to confer with the group. "How 'bout after we hit the beach, we get cleaned up, rest, then get dressed and eat at Claudia's, then go kick it at the Pelican Bar?"

The gang was all on board.

Winston pulled the van directly in front of the doors at the resort. A trio wearing white pants and turquoise shirts stood off to the side; they were playing ska music. Two servers greeted us with warm smiles and colorful drinks that had small umbrellas in them. Each of us took a drink then proceeded to the front desk to check in.

We were set once everyone got their cards. "Aight, y'all, see you back here in thirty minutes." With those words, Carl and I headed to our bungalow.

Brooke

While Seven and I followed the bellhop to our bungalow, my eyes were fixed on the pristine white sand and waves running ashore only steps away from our door. In my spirit, I felt this trip was going to be ultra-special.

I thought I'd died and gone to heaven when the bellhop opened the door. Luxurious marble floors were throughout. It had plush, gray sofas, a 70" flat-screen television on the wall, a fully stocked bar, a king-size canopy bed with sheer sheets all around it, and a Magnum with a bucket of Moet on ice on the nightstand. The bathroom had an enclosed, glass-case shower, toilet, double vanity, and an alfresco clawfoot tub in a private area outside in the back. If ever there was a paradise, I had just stumbled into it.

I kicked off my sneakers and fell back on the bed with my hands above my head. "Aaah!" I sighed aloud. The bed was super soft and comfortable. Seven chuckled at my reaction.

"Looks like you ready to vacation."

"Yesss! This resort is everything."

He glanced around the room. "It really is stunning, but not nearly as stunning as you, beautiful." He gave me that look like *you can get it*.

I blushed.

Seven walked over and laid on top of me. We began to passionately kiss. I sensed he wanted to get things popping, but I broke away from his soft lips.

"Now, you know if we get started, neither of us will want to stop, so I suggest we wait til we come back from the beach."

He knew I was right, so he got up.

"I do have something you can have now, tho," I flirtatiously stated.

His face lit up with a beaming smile. "Oh, yeah? What you got for me?"

I walked over to my Louis Vuitton purse and pulled out a piece of folded paper. I handed it to him. His facial expression changed from lust and excitement to curiosity.

"What's this?" He unfolded and skimmed over it. "So, your divorce is finalized?"

Smiling, I nodded my head.

He wrapped his arms around me and kissed me. "Good. Now you're officially my woman."

"I'm officially yours, baby," I replied happily, looking into his eyes.

We joined the others in the lobby, then headed to the main dining hall for brunch. The hall was spacious and opulent. Nicely decorated white cloth tables and chairs surrounded a buffet that was large enough to feed an army. It was stocked with fresh fruit, breakfast foods, sandwiches, and different kinds of salads. I got a few strips of turkey bacon, hash browns, a veggie omelet, and a bowl of chopped fruit. Seven's plate was loaded with scrambled eggs, sausage links, and biscuits and gravy. We ate out on the patio by the pool. A view of the ocean was in the backdrop.

We were ready to get the day going with the first activity after everyone satisfied their hunger pangs, so we went back to our bungalows to prepare for the beach. Seven changed into yellow trunks and a wife-beater. His beautiful locs were braided back into a man-bun. Keeping it sexy and cute, I put on a royal blue, twopiece bikini with gold rings on the top and hips. I wrapped a blue, sheer sarong around my waist. I double checked my beach bag, then put on my black, Gucci sunglasses, and we left out.

Carmen and Will were the only couple at the rendezvous spot on the walkway. She had on a sexy, black and white striped onepiece swimsuit with three peepholes down the middle, a floppy, straw hat, and dark, Versace shades covering her eyes. Carmen had a nice figure; you'd never suspect she had recently given birth to her fourth child.

Will was a big guy. He had played college football but didn't stay in shape when those days were over. He had on blue trunks and a tank-top.

"Your bikini is cute, Brooke!" said Carmen.

"Thank you. Yours, too. I'm loving that hat, girl!" I replied. "I see we the only ones on time."

"Ain't nothing changed with them two."

Seconds later, Hanifa and Jahsani were walking towards us. Hanifa was wearing a fuchsia, two-piece, drawstring bikini and a white sarong around her waist, and was carrying a beach bag. Her braids were in a ponytail. Jahsani had on black trunks and a black wife-beater.

Hanifa asked, "Where's Michaela and Carl?"

"I'm sure they'll pop up any second now," I answered. "I like that color on you, 'Nifa."

"Thanks. Y'all look cute," she responded. "Ooh, Carmen... ain't no way you look that good six months after having your fourth child."

"Thank you. I'm trying to make time so I can workout with Brooke and Michaela to preserve my sexy." She dropped it twice like it was hot. "Aye, aye!"

Michaela and Carl walked up while we were laughing at Carmen's antics. They looked like they had just come off the set of a Beenie Man video shoot. Michaela wore a red, yellow, and green, two-piece, g-string bikini with a black, net gown over it in addition, she had on a pair of dark Gucci sunglasses. Carl had on green trunks. His shirt was tied around his head like a turban. I guess he wanted to show off his fit physique.

I couldn't resist the opportunity to tease Michaela. "I see you on yo' ill na-na shit!"

In true Michaela fashion, she twirled around and gave us a full view before responding in her best Jamaican accent, "What gwan? Mi come fi mash up dem island!"

We busted out laughing.

Hanifa spanked Michaela's butt. "Yo' ass done watched Shotta's one too many times." She smiled as she shook her head.

"What's up? Y'all ready to hit the beach?" Michaela was excited.

Everyone said 'yeah' or something to that effect in almost perfect unison.

As we made our way to the beach, all eyes were on us, and rightfully so. It was so much ass and titties bouncing and jiggling that it was hard to focus on anything else.

We secured our bags in the beach lockers, then went to get on the jet skis. Once we got out on the water, all the girls seemed to feel more comfortable and quickly got the hang of it. It was actually more fun than I anticipated.

Carmen challenged the guys to a race. It was the guys against the girls. Buoy to buoy. Losers would have to take a double shot of tequila later when we went out... but there was one condition – they guys had to give me, Michaela, and Hanifa a three links head start. They accepted the bet without hesitation.

Carl and Michaela were the first couple up. Seven called it out. "On your mark. Get set. GO!" the two took off, skipping across the water at high speeds toward the buoy, 200 yards away. Michaela turned around and raised her arms, indicating she won.

Next up were Hanifa and Jahsani. Carmen and I cheered her on, hoping to boost her confidence. Seven called it out. "On your mark. Get set. GO!" The two took off, streaking across the water until Jahsani's arms raised in victory. It was now tied up.

Will and Carmen were next. Their race was heads-up because she was an experienced rider. Once again, Seven called it out. "On your mark. Get set. GO!" The two of them took off like rockets. As they zipped across the waters, you could easily tell they were both far from beginners. Unfortunately, Will squeaked by Carmen and raised his hands. The score was two to one in favor of the guys.

It was all on me. Seven was an experienced rider, so I knew my only real chance to steal the win was to get an early takeoff and hope like hell I outran him. I could feel Seven's presence behind me as I took my three links head start. I raised up and wiggled my booty in front of him.

"I got something on my butt. Can you see it?"

He started to laugh. "I see you trying to distract me with them chocolate cakes!"

"Is it working?"

"A little," he laughed. He paused as he tried to get serious and countdown the start of the race.

"On your mark...

"Get set..."

I took off before he said 'go'. He gave chase. As I skipped along the water, a slight mist kicked up in my face and mouth. The saltwater's taste was bitter.

I had the throttle back as far as my grip would allow, but Seven quickly caught up and was on my side. I could see the girls cheering for me the closer we got to the finish line. We were about twenty yards from the buoy when Seven deaccelerated, allowing me to pull ahead and cross first. The girls celebrated my victory, but I knew he let me win.

For 45 minutes, we jet skied around the part of the island near the resort. We then went and chilled on the beach. After laying out in the sun with the girls for a while, I went and joined Seven in the water. The water was warm but got cooler the further we drifted out. The girls sat at the foot of the shoreline, enjoying the waves that came rolling in on them.

There we were, in the ocean, with my legs wrapped around him in a warm embrace, enjoying a picturesque moment. As I looked into his eyes, I could see the sun's reflection.

"That was sweet of you to let me win out there."

He didn't try to downplay or deny it. "Brooke, I'll always put you and Yasmin first. Always," he reiterated.

His response prompted me to kiss him. I didn't mind that his lips tasted like the bitter saltwater.

As the waves rolled in, we bobbed and drifted, and I was slowly becoming aroused by his dick rubbing against my mound. His dick was getting harder by the second. I yearned to feel it inside of me.

"This water feels good," he stated.

No one was around to hear us, so I thought it was the perfect opportunity for a quickie. I looked into his eyes. "You know what else feels good?" I sensually asked.

"What's that, baby?"

I rested my forehead on his. "When you put that big dick inside me and hit my spot over and over again."

"Is that right?"

"Yes, but it feels even better when I'm cummin' all on that big dick." I bit my bottom lip as I imagined the sensational feeling.

We started kissing. He slid my bikini to the side and guided his dick inside of me. "Ummm," I purred in delight as the initial discomfort turned into pleasure.

He was being discreet with minimum movement, yet he pelvic stroked me slow and deep. Each stroke massaged my clit. It felt like he was pushing up into my stomach. I sucked on his neck to muffle my moans. As the sensation intensified, so did Seven's pace and force.

"Don't stop... don't stop," I moaned. He tilted me back to get a better range of motion. It worked. He started going deeper. "Oooh, Seven... I'm cummin', baby... I'm cummiiin'!" I uttered in a low, sultry tone.

But he wasn't done with me. His grip on my butt got stronger. "That's it... cum all over it, baby," he heavily panted.

"I'm cummin' all over it," I cooed, basking in the throes of ecstasy.

"Oooh, Brooke..."

The way he said my name, I knew he was about to explode.

He buried it all the way in me and let out a deep grunt. "Aaah... aaaaah!"

It took everything in me not to scream out loud.

He laid inside of me as we drifted. The mystique of the ocean made me feel super relaxed, like I'd taken a sedative. The others were ready to go get cleaned up, so we made our way back in, emerging from the surf without anyone knowing what just happened.

When we got back to the bungalow, we cuddled on the hammock. We relaxed, talked, and acted silly with one another. We did this for about two hours, at which time we went inside and took a shower together.

Everything about Seven's naked body turned me on. His arms, muscular chest, the tattoo of a black ankh that covered his vshaped back, and all that dick. *Mmm, it looks like a root beer bomb pop waiting to be sucked on.*

Although the sun was beginning its descent, the outside temperature was a pleasant 80°, so I put on a multi-colored maxidress, thong sandals, and sprayed on a mist of my new favorite perfume by Tom Ford. I was moisturizing my face in front of the mirror when Seven walked by and stopped.

"You smell great, baby." He placed his hand around my waist and kissed my neck."

Blushing, I replied, "Thank you."

He had on red Cargo shorts, a black and red t-shirt, and black sandals. He was irrefutably handsome. I managed to get a whiff of his cologne; it was the same from earlier.

"What's that you're wearing?" I flirtatiously asked.

"YSL."

"I love it. It's sexy."

"Duly noted."

Surprisingly, we were the last couple to the lobby. Winston was outside waiting for us. We went and loaded into the van, ready to experience Claudia's.

We rolled along the winding road and enjoyed the beautiful view of the coastline. We then headed up into the hillside where small houses and shacks were tucked back from the road. once on the other side of the hill, we came upon the bustling section of town. People were moving around. Some hanging out in front of shops, and some sitting in old chairs on vacant lots. All seemed to be enjoying the day.

Winston pulled over and parked in front of a green and white storefront with a sign on the window that read *Claudia's Kitchen, Authentic Jamaican Cuisine.* One by one, we filed into the restaurant.

Claudia's wasn't a huge establishment, but it was nice. The locals inside were talking and enjoying their food. A top-heavy, brown-skinned woman came over and greeted us. Her accent was stronger than Winston's.

"Hello, Winston. Who do we have here?"

"Good people from the States looking for the real taste of Jamaica. You know me have to bring them to ya."

She smiled at us. "Welcome to Claudia's. I'm Claudia, and me got the best food pon the island! Me gon' take real good care of ya." As she spoke, two workers combined tables so we could all sit together. "Today's special is crispy jerk chicken rolls wit' cho cho slaw, and coconut-crusted, grouper fillets and steamed cassava bammy" she informed us, ready to take our orders.

Seven and I ordered opposite dishes so we could share and sample a larger variety. While waiting on our food, we talked about all the fun we had jet skiing earlier and made plans for what we would do the next day. Will suggested snorkeling, but the hair divas did not want to get their hair wet. Carl suggested zip lining. After briefly mulling it over, we all agreed to it and decided 1pm should be the meetup time.

Claudia and two others brought out our orders. Everything looked and smelled fabulous. The coconut-crusted grouper was delicious. It was flaky and tasty. The highpoint of the meal, however, were the jerk chicken rolls, which were unquestionably amazing!

With our bellies full and darkness settling in, it was time to hang out and have some drinks. Claudia came to clear our table.

"How was every ting?"

Carl answered quickly. "Ms. Claudia, I'm gon' need you to mail me some of your jerk chicken rolls to Atlanta. They were delicious!"

"Yeah, mon!" replied Claudia with a huge smile.

I asked her if she'd take a picture with us.

"Sure."

I handed Winston my phone, making him the photographer. We then all bunched together for the picture. Afterwards, I paid for our meals and left a $40 tip. We returned to the van and left. Feeling good, of course.

Winston drove to the westside of the island so we could get on a water taxi and go to Floyd's. We arrived at the boat slip just in time. People had just started to board the boat. Excited and ready to turn up, we hurriedly jumped in line.

The boat went out about a mile to Parottee Bay before reaching Floyd's Pelican Bar, which turned out to be a quirky, driftwood shack on stilts and a sandbar. The sounds of a live band playing reggae music filled the night air as we walked up to the bar. People were all about – standing, talking, dancing, drinking, and enjoying themselves. This was definitely the spot for us. We made our way over to the bar. Carmen got the attention of a pretty, West Indian woman with long, black hair and a sexy accent like Winston's.

"What can I get for ya?" she asked.

"We don't want no rum drinks!" Carmen specified. "What would you recommend that will have me and my friends lit?"

The bartender smiled. "Me know just the ting for ya." She then mixed a concoction in a tumbler, shook it vigorously, and strained it eight times. "It's called a Time Bomb."

"Why you call it a time bomb?" asked Hanifa.

"Cuz it gon' sneak up on ya, then boom!" she said, flashing her hand like it blew up.

We all quickly and curiously took sips to taste it. It was nice.

Carmen loved it. "Now that's what I'm talking about right there!" She then paid for the drinks as we started to walk off. She quickly stopped us. "Hold up," she said, looking at the guys, "y'all lost the bet earlier, so y'all supposed to do a double-shot."

The guys confusingly looked at one another. Will shook his head. "How is that when the score was two to two?"

"Because all ties go to the ladies!" Carmen answered.

The guys all laughed. Will said, "You just made that up."

Carl quickly weighed in. "Tell you what, since it was a tie, everyone should do a double-shot."

Michaela looked at him with a huge grin on her face. "Y'all trying to get us turnt up so y'all can take advantage of us, huh?"

The guys looked at each other, then back at us, and in unison resoundingly responded, "Hell yeah!"

We were on vacation and committed to making it a memorable one, so we went along and did a double shot of Patron with them. Little did we know, every round of drinks would come with a double shot, too.

The live band's female and male singers performed renditions of reggae royalty like Dawn Penn's classic hit *No, No, No* and Sasha's *I'm Still in Love With You*, giving off the island's true cultural vibe. We were all grooving and having a good time, but two hours and three rounds later, the Time Bombs detonated. At that time, the band was playing more sensual dancehall songs like Mad Cobra's *Flex* and Little Twitch's *Touch*. What began as a cool rock and sway morphed into provocative gyration by practically everyone on the dance floor. Basically, we were having sex with our clothes on.

Michaela expertly twerked on Carl, showing the local competition how the A-Town gets down. Carmen gave a local couple a run for their money with the way she was whinin' on Will. Hanifa and Jahsani were grinding so nasty it looked like she might conceive any moment. And me, I was slow whinin' with my back to Seven. His hands, caressing my waist and hips and thighs, sent sexual currents racing throughout my body. I felt the bulge of his penis through the thin material of my dress as I grinded against it.

The band's live session ended at midnight, so we left the bar and boarded the boat. Winston was waiting for us at the dock. We were tipsy and modestly drunk, so the ride back to the resort was a quiet one.

Michaela and Carl, along with Seven and I, were ready to call it a night. The others, however, wanted to hang out a bit longer. With them having children, this was understandable. They didn't get out too often. This night, they were going to make every second count.

It was a romantic, starry night. The ambient sounds of the island provided a sensual soundtrack. Seven and I removed our sandals and strolled along the shoreline, reveling in the majesty of the moon's gravitational pull on the ocean as the tide rolled in on our feet and retracted. We came upon our bungalow. Seven stood behind me and wrapped his arms around my body. We stared out at the ocean. The sound of his voice broke the silence.

"Brooke, there's something I've been wanting to say to you since we got to Jamaica, but I'm just now finding the words to express it," he calmly stated.

I turned around to face him. "What's on your mind, baby?" "From the moment I laid eyes on you, my spirit was drawn to you like a moth is to a flame. The joy and peace I feel when I'm with you is undeniable, like it is right now. I've never experienced a connection this deep with any other woman. What I'm getting at is this, I know your divorce just got finalized, and I'm not trying to rush you, but I want all of you, baby, and that includes you being my wife... my queen."

The gaze in his eyes awakened feelings in me I'd tucked away and forgotten about years ago. I had gotten used to being left speechless by Seven, but tonight I was like a deer caught in headlights. I wanted to respond, but was unable to get a word out of my mouth.

Seven was the kind of man I always dreamt of spending my life with. He was the kind of man I could give all of myself to... with no regrets. I wanted to respond. I needed to respond. I did respond.

"I feel the same way about you, Seven. You're everything I need and want in a man. You inspired me to confront my fears, to own my greatness, and above all you've given me the courage to love again and to be loved." I paused, for my emotions had caused my voice to crack. "My heart is in your hands. All I ask is, if there's something I'm not doing that you would like for me to do, tell me, teach me, and I promise I'll do my best to make you happy."

Like two magnetic forces, our lips came together in a passionate kiss. He swooped me off my feet and carried me inside. He put me down in front of the dresser. Heavily inebriated, I leaned up against the wall and turned around so he could untie the drawstring fastened around my neck.

His big body pinned me against the wall. His hands went under my dress. They traveled up my legs until he realized I didn't have any panties to pull down. "That's how you feel," he whispered in my ear as he helped me out of the dress.

After fumbling with his belt, I heard his shorts hit the floor. Suddenly, his huge hands pinned mine to the wall. I then felt his supple lips kissing on my shoulders and neck. I panted in anticipation of the pleasure to come.

He pressed his knee into the back of mine, causing me to spread my legs. He teased me with the head until my wetness soaked the tip. Inch by inch, he slowly inserted it until I winced. "Sssss! Oh my, God... I love all this dick, baby." I was convinced that there was no better feeling in the world.

With a full range of motion, he slowly and fluidly stroked. His dick magic applied such a significant stimulation to my clit that a tingly sensation built up. He changed his stroke to a deep, upward one. It was like he was scooping ice cream with his dick.

"Baby... baby... oooh!" I screamed in delight of the bliss reverberating throughout my body.

He whispered in my ear, "I want you on the bed," and then he pulled out.

The reward of ecstasy ran down my thigh.

Before getting on the bed, I knelt and put his dick in my mouth. In and out I sucked, savoring the sweetness of my nectar that clung to it. "That feels great, baby," he said. The faster I went, the wetter and sloppier it got, and also the wetter and hornier I became. I slowly worked my way up, then positioned myself on the bed on my hands and knees. Face down. Ass up.

Seven reinserted his dick and began long stroking me in a way that made it feel like his manhood was a foot long when he retracted. Within minutes, my walls began contracting for another explosive orgasm.

It had been a long time since I had been fucked in the ass. At that moment, I strongly felt the urge for anal penetration. Panting heavily, I looked back at Seven and told him to take it out and put it in my ass.

Trying to steady his breathing, Seven replied, "If I do, I'm gon' cum quick."

"Good. So will I."

He continued stroking, massaging my asshole with his thumb. He slipped a finger in to see how tight it was. He worked up to two fingers and a distant feeling resurfaced. "Yesss!" I cooed. Sensing I was ready, he withdrew his fingers and teased my asshole with the tip of his meaty head, then slowly eased it in. I instantly tensed up. I reached back, impeding him from going any further. He was too big for me to let him dictate how much dick he'd put inside me, so I took control.

Cautiously, I pressed back against it until I could no longer take any more. I had about three inches inside of me. "Right there," I said, letting him know the limit. Within seconds of him moving in and out, my ass got wetter, and the pleasurable sensation intensified tenfold.

Seven's breathing turned into heavy panting as he increased the pace, causing my moans to grow even louder. "Yes, yes... hit that ass, baby! Hit it!" I commanded as my asshole constricted around his dick so tight that he couldn't move it or pull it out. I sat there and convulsed uncontrollably from the exhilarating sensation of cummin'.

My spasmatic trembling triggered Seven's explosion. "Ooh, shit! Shit, shit, shit!" he groaned. I felt his dick pulsate as it exploded inside of me.

The softening of Seven's dick from the orgasm, and the creamy filling of my asshole, allowed Seven to get his dick from inside of me. When it came out, I collapsed on the bed. I laid there and trembled for over three minutes as orgasm after orgasm erupted. I came so hard that I passed out.

Chapter 11

(Michaela)

Awakened from the tropical breeze blowing in off the ocean, I shivered and opened my eyes. The high of last night's sexual proclivities were slowly wearing off. I looked up and realized we had left the sliding door open all night.

On the nightstand beside me was the magnum with a bottle of Moet floating on melted ice. I slipped out of the bed and poured me a glass of champagne. I then padded across the cool, marble floor to retract the sliding door to a modest crack. Standing there naked sipping champagne, I took in the beauty of the beachfront ocean view, enjoying the effects of paradise. There was no stress about work, finding the perfect house, or even a single thought about Dee Dee.

I don't know if it was the alcohol or all the fun we had yesterday, but Carl showed his ass. When we got in last night, he took off my clothes, hoisted me against the wall and fucked me like there was no tomorrow. Then he passed out.

While finishing my champagne, I looked back at Carl's naked body. He was still asleep. A sense of gratitude for him being in my life came over me. My buzz had been reignited and I was ready to play. It was his birthday, and I had my mind set on making it one he would always remember.

Carl's dick was so big that even when soft it was still meaty and tempting. Stealthily, I positioned myself opposite of him and nestled up close to his crotch. Without using my hands, I licked the head up and down his flaccid dick. He didn't flinch. I sucked the head into my mouth and began contracting my jaws; his dick started to swell up. Within two minutes, I had resuscitated it to last night's glory.

I slowly stuffed his dick in my mouth. I slurped and goggled as I licked and sucked. He woke up, blurry-eyed and surprised.

"Oh, it's lit," he said in a low, morning voice.

"Um-hm," I moaned, then pulled it out my mouth and licked up and down the shaft.

Now that my audience of one had his eyes on me, I was overly anxious to put on a show. I sucked one of his balls while stroking his dick at the same time. I placed my fingertips around the head, gently kneading it, then formed a circle with my thumb and forefinger and slid it up and down while swirling my tongue around the shaft.

Wide-eyed, he laid there and gasped. I slowly stuffed his dick, inch by inch, into my mouth until it was in my throat. I then slurped and sucked as I retracted like I was trying to snatch his soul out his body. "Goddamn!" he rejoiced in proverbial delight.

It was no secret that I was having fun. I flickered my tongue in his pee hole while stroking, jerking up and down, hard and quick. I was trying to pump the nut out of his dick.

"Ooh, shit! Here it comes, Michaela!" he forewarned in a deep moan before erupting like a volcano.

I tried to catch as much as I could but it was just too much. He stared as I rolled my tongue over my lips, savoring every drop that got away.

"Ooh, baby, you a monster!" he emphatically declared, fully satisfied.

Fueled by the show, he tossed my leg over his body. We were now in the 69 position. He spread my cheeks apart with his thumbs and fingers. I felt the flat of his tongue lick from my clit to my asshole, then back to my clit. I let out a high-pitch moan, "Ooooh!"

The moistness of his tongue rimming my asshole sent chills and thrills up my spine. (Damn, I love the freak in him). He alternated between my pussy and asshole, licking lasciviously with equal delight. I moaned feverishly.

My body began to tingle by the intensity of the surfeit sensation building up inside of me. I could tell right away this was going to be a big one. I grounded myself closer to his mouth and began gyrating in small circles. The faster I sucked and slurped on his dick, the more he licked and slurped on my clit.

"Yes... eat that pussy, daddy... eat it!" I vociferously uttered.

All of a sudden, my eyes began fluttering. Strobes of colorful lights flashed like a kaleidoscope as my body went into a tumultuous convulsion.

Swoosh!!

Swoosh!!

Swoosh!!

My orgasm shot out in three waves like a waterfall. Carl's face, neck, and chest were soaked in my juices. I could hear him moaning and hungrily lapping it up. The euphoria of the intense eruption left me momentarily paralyzed. My eyes flitted back and forth, trying desperately to focus on something. Unable to collect myself, I collapsed face-first on the bed between his legs.

Carl caught his second wind and was hard again. He got up and walked away. I could hear him rummaging through his shower bag. Seconds later, I felt a few drops hit my butt. He smeared it all over my cheeks, working up to my asshole, where he massaged it in with a finger. I knew then it was K-Y Jelly.

He guided his dick inside of my sopping, wet pussy and began stroking, slowly building up to deep plunges. I felt another orgasm building up in a matter of minutes. The sound of him slamming into the globes of my ass made a rhythmic, clapping sound.

"Carl, I'm cummin'... I'm cummin', baby" I screamed as another orgasm unfurled.

He quickly withdrew and slowly worked the head into my asshole. He pumped in and out with shallow strokes. This only intensified my orgasm.

"Oh my, God... gimme more, daddy... gimme more!" I begged.

Carl granted my request. He increased the pace while I rubbed on my clit. I didn't think I had anything left to give, but then I felt another one coming on, and it was more intense than the others. I grabbed two fistfuls of sheets to brace myself, then screamed as my entire body started to shake.

"Oh my, God... oh my, God!!"

Swoosh!!

Swoosh!!

Swoosh!!

Another tsunami.

The electrifying sensation was so powerful that it turned my screams of pleasure into tears of joy. I couldn't help but to cry.

"Uaahh!" groaned Carl as he exploded and collapsed on my back while I laid there sobbing and shaking uncontrollably until we both drifted back to sleep.

I thought I was dreaming when I heard what sounded like a phone ringing. It rang again, but this time it sounded louder, bringing me out of my slumber. Woozy from the cataleptic effects of multiple, squirting orgasms, I reached out and managed to snag enough of the cord to pull the receiver off the base and then reel it in.

"Hello?" I answered in a groggy voice.

"Girl, I know yo' early bird ass ain't still sleep."

"Hanifa? What time is it?" My voice faded in and out.

"Ooh, Carl must've murdered you last night because you sound out of it! It's 12 o'clock."

We'd been asleep for four hours. I started drifting back to sleep.

"Michaela!" yelled Hanifa. "Girl, get up. We're supposed to be leaving in an hour."

"I am." I was still out of it.

She yelled my name again. "Michaela!"

I exhaled.

"Girl, get up!"

"I'm up, I'm up. Please, stop yelling."

"Carmen and Will just came down to eat, so we're all sitting out by the pool."

"Aight. We'll be down in a few."

I put the phone back on the base and took a deep breath. Carl rolled over and spanked my right butt cheek.

"Getcho ass up, Etta Mae!" he said, impersonating Ike Turner.

I didn't have enough strength to laugh, but I did chuckle. "Bae, cut the shower on for me please."

"I gotchu." He kissed the globes of my ass as he got out of the bed.

Once I heard the shower running, I garnered enough strength to get up. I was still woozy, so I checked to make sure my legs were under me, then went and joined Carl in the shower.

I started to wake up as soon as the hot water hit my body. After showering, I put on some green fashion leggins, a white tank-top, green and black and white Nike Air Max sneakers, and a pair of dark Gucci sunglasses. Carl put on some baggy, black basketball shorts, a wife-beater, and a pair of Retro Jordan sneakers.

Due to the excessive amount of fluids released, my stomach was growling and I was in desperate need of sustenance and hydration. We made our way to the dining hall, fixed a plate, then joined the others out on the patio by the pool. Hanifa handed me Brooke's phone so I could see how we were dancing last night. I burst out laughing when I saw Carmen and Will, and Hanifa and Jahsani, too.

"Y'all was out there getting it like young pussy cats!" I remarked. "Damn, Jahsani, you might have blue balls 'cause y'all was grinding hella hard," I teased.

Carmen quickly clapped back. "Of all people... I know you ain't talking 'bout nobody, Ms. Twerk-a-licious!"

"What you talking about?" I asked, clueless to what she was referring to.

"Just keep watching the video, you'll see what I'm talking 'bout."

The video showed me and Carl. I was shocked to see myself twerking and whinin' on him with one leg on his hip while he was giving it back to me. Carl and I broke out laughing.

"Aye, I had to show them girls dancing next to us how we do it in the A," I said while configuring my fingers to make an A.

I devoured the first of two egg and sausage sandwiches I made. Brooke must've read my energy because she looked at me and shook her head, smiling.

"What?" I asked.

"What happened to you this morning, Ms. Thang? It ain't like you to sleep late."

I lowered my sunglasses and gave her a look that signified I'd gotten my brains fucked out.

"I know the feeling," she mumbled, laughing.

The other's looked refreshed and excited for the day, especially Carmen. She wished Carl a happy birthday and asked, "How does it feel to be the old man in the group?"

Everyone else wished him a happy birthday, not knowing I had blown out his candle four hours ago.

Carl responded, "Old...? I'm only six years older than y'all."

"Exactly," Carmen shot back.

"Don't pay her no mind, baby. You look great to be 42." I leaned over and kissed him.

Hanifa just had to say something. "Aww... ain't that sweet? She came to the aid of her man."

"That part! Don't be trying to come for my baby," I playfully responded.

Brooke glanced at her watch and joined the conversation. "So, what's the plan for today?"

I swallowed my food and washed it down with freshly squeezed papaya juice. "We agreed to go zip lining at one. While in the mountains, I propose we check out the blue lagoon, then hit the town and do a little shopping at the local shops. That'll give us enough time to come back and rest up or go do something on your own before the dinner party tonight at 9pm at Bailey's on the beach."

"That sounds cool," said Brooke. She looked around the table to see if there were any objections.

It was now 1pm. "Is everyone ready, or do you need to go get anything?" I asked.

Everyone said they were ready, so we headed toward the front. Winston and another driver were talking when we walked outside.

"Good afternoon, ladies. What's up, fellas? Ya ready?" he asked.

"Let's do it," answered Carl as we filed into the van.

"Where to, Ms. Jackson?"

"We're going zip lining, then we would like to see the Blue Lagoon on Blue Mountain, and then go into town so we can do some shopping," I instructed.

Twenty minutes later, Winston turned the van into a lush rainforest along Strawberry Hill's Zip Lining Trail. We exited the van and checked in at the cabin. A dark-skinned man gave us a safety speech about equipment and the proper way to zip line. Once he finished, we set out on a winding trail and hiked up the mountain for fifteen minutes. By the time we reached the zip line, we were able to look over some trees.

The instructor handed us helmets and asked who was going first. We hesitantly looked at each other to see who was brave enough to go down first. After a few quiet stares, Seven stepped forward. "I'll set it off," he said. The guys began high-fiving him. He kissed Brooke, then secured the harness around his waist and crotch. He stepped up on the platform, took a deep breath, then pushed off and zipped down until he disappeared into the rainforest.

Brooke was next by default. She secured the harness and called out to the ancestors to watch over her. She pushed off and screamed as she slid down the cable. We could still hear her after she disappeared into the rainforest.

Seeing Brooke zip line gave me the courage to go next. My heartbeat like it was about to jump out of my chest as I secured the harness. I took a deep breath and pushed off. I screamed like a little girl as the zip line picked up speed.

Once I got through the trees, I saw Brooke and Seven. They were both laughing while she recorded me on her phone. The adrenaline rush made me feel excited and aroused. It was the third exhilarating feeling I had experienced that day.

"Girl, you gotta see the face you was making!"

"That shit was crazy!" I excitedly replied to Brooke.

Minutes later, Carl came zipping through the trees. The looks on everyone's faces as they appeared out the trees was priceless. Luckily, Brooke was able to capture every moment. She texted the videos to our phones so we would always have footage of the memories close by.

We headed to the front and loaded in the van to our next destination. While en route to the mountain, everyone shared her/his experience of zip lining. Hanifa's trumped all others. She claimed that when she pushed off, her left breast almost flopped out of her bra. Carmen thought she was going to pee on herself. I shared that the thrill made my nipples get hard.

The fellas swore they weren't affected by the adrenaline rush, but we knew that wasn't true. A replay of the video revealed that each hollered as he came through the tree line.

As we drove into the hills, we began to see people in swimsuits, shorts, and flip-flops with towels draped around their necks. They walked along the side of the road looking satisfyingly wet.

"Where are they coming from, Winston?" asked Jahsani.

"People hang out and swim in the cool stream that flows down the mountain. Some parts are deeper than the others, like this spot here," he pointed to a trail several people were trekking. "It's about five feet deep there."

"How far is it from where we're going?"

"Just around the bend up ahead."

"Can we walk from here?"

"Sure, if that's what you'd like."

Winston pulled off the road and parked in the grass. We exited the van and followed him along a beaten path into the brush. The smell of marijuana being smoked and fruit bread cooking filled the air. The closer we got, the louder the sounds of reggae music playing on a radio were. We could also hear people talking and laughing, and kids playing in the water.

The path opened up to a flowing stream. Kids and adults were playing in the shallow waters while some teenagers hung out on the cliffs on the other side of the stream. Another group was downstream swinging on a rope tied to a branch. They were jumping into the deeper end. A small group of people in front of us had a rock fire going under a pot cooking fruit bread.

Seeing how relaxed and carefree the people were as they enjoyed their favorite pastimes helped me understand why some folks don't care for the daily hassles of living in a big city. They seemed happy and content without designer clothes and fancy automobiles and expensive jewelry and tall buildings and titles.

When we reached the area near the bend in the trail, we encountered a wooden bridge that crossed over the stream. I grabbed ahold of the rope rail and carefully followed Winston to the other side. We walked along another trail for a few minutes before the sounds of gushing waters were heard. The brush suddenly opened up, and I saw the most beautiful thing I'd ever laid eyes on in my 35 years of living.

A lovely waterfall cascaded down into an aqua-blue lagoon. The surrounding light-blue, red, purple, and white orchids looked like a living postcard. Other tourists were along the banks taking pictures and enjoying the scenery. The island's beaches and shorelines may be the initial draws, but hidden gems like the cascading waterfall are the island's best kept secret.

Carl hugged me from behind as we reveled over the hypnotic visual. "How beautiful is this?" he calmly asked. "Baby, it's amazing!" I replied, enthralled.

Winston pointed to an area over the mountain up ahead where local mystics, naturalists, and Rastafarians went to meditate, chant, and connect with nature. He said it's believed that the electromagnetic field of Blue Mountain stimulates higher consciousness, prompting people to flock there every morning.

Hanifa closed her eyes like she was channeling. "I can feel it," she said, holding her chest.

"Feel what?" asked Carmen.

"The energy," Hanifa replied. "Water is the greatest conductor of electricity, so the energy surrounding the waterfall, the stream, and trees is highly charged. Look at the top of the mountain," she instructed, pointing. "See that bluish-looking halo outlining the mountain?"

Carmen answered, "Yeah, I see it."

"That's the energy field surrounding the mountain. The higher the energy, the brighter the color. Purple is the highest, based on the spectrum of light we can physically see."

"That's crazy!" said Carmen, clearly amazed at what she saw and learned.

Everyone began taking pictures. We took group pictures, couples' pictures, all girls' pictures, and all guys' pictures. Altogether, we spent over an hour on the mountain before making our way back down to the van.

"I don't think anything can top that," I said to the group as Winston pulled off.

"You might be right, Michaela," said Brooke, "that was breathtaking."

Winston dropped us off at the square, where local vendors sold souvenirs and merchandise under tents. Young children were walking up and down the sidewalks; they advertised everything from bottled waters to fruits and vegetables, t-shirts and handmade jewelry to battery ran handheld fans. We patronized several vendors, then made our way to the main shopping district.

I bought a novelty set of shot glasses in the first shop we ventured into. The glasses immediately caught my eye because of the words etched into them. One said Peter Meter, and the other said Pum Pum Meter.

We entered a shop a couple of doors down that specialized in aromatherapy candles, herbal concoctions, and an array of fine, handcrafted jewelry made from raw and polished stones and crystals. Hanifa and Brooke flew up and down the aisles picking up things like two witches on broomsticks. They connected with the shop's owner, Mrs. Ieolla, a caramel-complected woman with beautiful salt and pepper locs. I bought Carl a malachite bracelet for his birthday and as a reminder of the trip.

We continued going in and out of shops. A particular shop caught Seven's attention, so we crossed the street to enter it. Its windows were filled with sculptures and paintings. Once inside, we saw a vast collection of hand carved woodworks: African masks, statues, bowls, walking sticks, eloquent incense holders, and ash trays.

One piece caused Seven to stop in his tracks. It was a beautiful coffee table with detailed carvings of animals up and down the table legs. Seven called the shopkeeper over. The shopkeeper was a clean-shaven, neatly dressed, West Indian man who wore wireframed glasses. Seven inquired about the table, its maker and the price. The artist passed away, and the price was $1600. Seven whipped out his wallet and handed the man a credit card. He asked if it could be shipped to his address. The shopkeeper was delighted to do so.

Three hours later, we were low on energy and ready to head back so we could eat and relax. We made our way to the van and Winston drove us to the resort.

As soon as I opened the door to mine and Carl's bungalow, I could tell housekeeping had been there. The fresh scent of some freshener was in the air, the bed was made with clean linens, and the trash can was emptied. I took my shoes off and opened the sliding door to allow some fresh air in. Carl relaxed on the sofa eating a burger.

"How you feel, birthday boy?" I asked as I sat beside him to eat my salad.

"I feel good, thanks to you," he answered with a cunning smile. "You was on one this morning, wasn't you?"

"I was on one?" I acted shocked. "Nah, you was on one! Seriously tho, I miss having mornings like that. We used to get it in like that all the time, but lately it's like we're seeing less and less of each other, and it's killing me."

"I know, baby. I'll cut back on the OT."

"The past two days have been wonderful. Not only because we're in Jamaica, but because we've been together. I pray we get this house. I'm ready to have this morning every morning."

"Me, too, baby."

Time was winding down, so I took a shower and then proceeded to beautify myself. I stroked my face with the jade stone roller, then used a rice powder cleanser. Next, I exfoliated with an enzyme exfoliator to get rid of dead skin cells, rinsed my face with cold water, and patted it dry. I then applied a few drops of essential rose oil on my forehead and cheeks. I massaged in a face moisturizer. My skin felt fresh and clean. Lastly, I applied a Mele foundation that matched my melanin-rich skin tone, and brushed it in to a perfect blend.

Tonight's special occasion called for my secret weapon, Bal D Afrique, an amazing perfume by Byredo. I put on a white,off the shoulder body con dress and white sandals that tied around my calves.

I was in the mirror putting on the finishing touches of my eyeliner when Carl stepped out the bathroom with a towel around his waist.

"Daaaaamn!" he astonishedly exclaimed. "You looking real scrumptious right about now baby!" he licked his lips and groped himself.

This was the type of reaction I was going for. "Thank you, baby."

He then walked over and kissed my neck. He gave me a devilish grin. "Oops," he said, pretending his towel came loose on its own as it hit the floor. The sight of his stiffening dick made my mouth water and nipples to perk up. There was a stirring between my thighs.

"You better quit playing with me, Carl Williams, before we be late to your own dinner party." I stared at him in the mirror.

"To hell with dinner. What I want to eat is right here," he passionately stated.

His dick was now at full staff, and he was making it rear up. I turned around and faced him. We began kissing. I felt hot all over. It took all of my willpower to break away from his lips.

"Baby, we can't leave everyone hanging like that," I tried to reason. I grabbed ahold of his hard, magic stick and sucked the head. "But, please believe, when we get back tonight it's on and poppin'. And you can have me any..." I sucked the head. "And every..." I sucked the head again. "Way you want me, baby." I sucked it one last time, then turned around and finished my eyebrows.

Carl was left standing looking silly. "You just gon' tease'em like that? You ain't right, Michaela. This is cruel and unusual punishment."

"Get dressed, baby. We can't be late for your dinner party." I turned around and spanked him on his naked butt as he walked away.

Carl emerged from the bathroom twenty minutes later. He wore a white, two-piece, linen pants set. His open shirt showed his wife-beater. On his feet were white Nike Air Force 1s, and on his head was a classy, Panama hat slightly cocked to one side. His green eyes shimmered like emeralds.

I was blown away by how nice everyone looked when we got to the lobby. Will had on a two-piece, white, linen short set with white alligator sandals. Carmen wore a white jumpsuit and sandals. Hanifa had on a white maxi dress with sandals. Jahsani wore a white, two-piece, linen pants set with some Air Force 1s. Brooke had on a white romper with sandals, and Seven had on white shorts, a fitted short-sleeve shirt, and white Gucci crocodile loafers. I was confident you wouldn't find a better dressed party on the entire island.

By the look on Brooke's face, I could tell she was about to get started.

"Okay, sexy momma. You giving it to'em in yo' hoe'in hard costume!" she joked.

"Thank you," I replied and vogued. "Everyone looks so sexy and clean. We gotta take some pictures."

I stopped a resort worker walking by and asked if he'd take a few pictures of us. He happily assisted us.

We made our way down the beach to Bailey's, one of the eight 5-star restaurants at the resort. The maître de' escorted us outside were lit tiki torches led to an eloquently set table with magnum stands with champagne on ice at both ends. The fellas pulled out our chairs. The servers poured champagne in everyone's glass.

Tonight's special was broiled lobster tail, scallops, and asparagus. As we waited for our salads, the conversations flowed from every direction about our experiences on the trip, the funny things we'd seen and heard, and how beautiful the island was.

Hanifa got Seven's attention as the salads arrived. "Seven, what was it about that table that drew you to it?"

"It's the story it tells. You saw the craftsmanship in the details of the carvings. It takes a lot of time to bring that to life. The level of skill, vision, and discipline required of the artist is something you rarely see anymore."

"I would like to buy a few pieces of art for the spa and house, but how do I know if I'm getting a good price?"

Seven chewed his salad and washed it down with champagne. "First thing you need to know is that the less copies there are, the greater the demand. The greater the demand, the more it can cost. Ultimately, everything boils down to what a person is willing to pay to acquire it. For example, this glass," he said while holding up his drink, "to someone else it's just a glass, so it has no value to them, but to me it represents the amazing vacation I had in Jamaica with my lady and friends. See how the story associated with it adds value to the glass? Now, let's say someone who's never been to Jamaica wants to have this glass, then they'll pay whatever price I feel it will take for me to part ways with the symbol of my experience."

The logic of his example made sense to everyone.

"My advice to you, Hanifa, is that whenever you see something you like, you get it. How it makes you feel is all that matters. In a couple of weeks, the gallery is having a showcase entitled 'Black Love', and it's going to be some amazing art there. Everyone is invited, so I hope y'all come out."

We enjoyed the last showcase, so we were definitely going to support this event.

Several servers brought our food out and placed it in front of the respective persons who ordered it. As expected of a 5-star restaurant, the food was spectacular. We talked and laughed throughout dinner, enjoying the sound of the ocean washing ashore.

After we finished eating, the servers cleared the table and brought out a cake with a single burning candle. We began singing happy birthday to Carl and laughed the whole time. Right before he blew out the candle, all the guys called for a speech. Being a good sport, Carl stood up to quiet the small mob. He held his champagne glass up before speaking.

"What can I say... first off, I'm thankful to celebrate my 42nd birthday."

"Ase!" shouted Seven, Brooke, Hanifa, and Jahsani as they raised their glasses.

Carl continued. "I wanna thank all of y'all for coming to celebrate tonight with me and my baby. And I gotta shoutout my baby for making this the best birthday I ever had... but there's something I gotta be honest about."

Those words - 'there's something I gotta be honest about – caused me to feel concerned. I always thought we had a great way of communicating. What could he have to tell me?

"Michaela, I know you think I've been working 16 hours a day to help with the down payment on the house. The truth is that buying a house together is a huge commitment I'm not comfortable doing with you as my girlfriend."

Carl sat his glass on the table. He reached into his pocket and pulled out a small, black box, then got down on one knee and opened it. My heart started beating so fast I thought I was going into cardiac arrest. Shocked, I covered my open mouth with both hands.

"Baby, I been bussin' my ass to buy you this ring so we can buy a house together as husband and wife."

He held his hand out for mine. Although it trembled from excitement, I gave it to him.

"Michaela Jackson, will you marry me?"

I was so overwhelmed with joy that all I could do was nod my head as tears fell from my eyes.

"Is that a yes, baby?"

"Yes, baby! Yes!"

Carl placed a dazzling four-carat, solitaire diamond ring on my finger. I slightly bent over to kiss him. He stood up and we hugged. Everyone at the table was clapping and smiling, but the girls were dabbing their eyes with tissue to prevent their tears of joy from ruining their mascara.

"Congratulations, Michaela!" exclaimed Brooke as she ran up and hugged me.

Carl and I received hugs and congratulations from everyone. Immediately afterward, Seven proposed a toast. Everyone raised their glasses as he spoke.

"Here's to Black Love!"

"To Black Love!" everyone saluted.

Chapter 12

(Hanifa)

My cell phone's alarm went off at zero-dark-thirty (4:30am). Blurry eyed and slightly hungover, I grabbed it off the nightstand and silenced the alarm.

We'd only been asleep for a couple of hours. After Carl had proposed to Michaela, we ordered four more bottles of champagne and celebrated, which led to me and jahsani making passionate, drunken love until we passed out.

It was now time to get up so we could go up on the mountain for sunrise meditation. After hearing Winston talk about the locals' reverence for the mountain's spiritual frequency, I told Jahsani I wanted to experience it for myself. I put on black leggings, a Bob Marley t-shirt, and some sneakers, then brushed my teeth and washed my face. Jahsani put on some shorts, a tshirt, and sneakers, then went to the bathroom to get cleaned up.

We stopped by the dining hall to grab some fruit. We then went to the front desk and asked for a driver. The driver assigned to us was a short, dark-skinned man named Monty, whose locs were as long as Jahsani's. As soon as we got in the van, he turned around and asked, "Where to, ma'am?"

"We'd like to go up to Blue Mountain Lagoon where people meditate at," I answered.

He nodded his head in approval. "Not many guests request to go into the mountains, but seeing that you have, I'll ask if you want the real experience or just want to go to the lagoon?"

"What's the real experience?" I asked.

"A little further from the lagoon, a lot of bredren and sistren gather to meditate, chant, and pray."

I looked at Jahsani, and the look in his eyes said it all. "We want the real experience," I said, excited about the opportunity for another authentic Jamaican experience.

As Monty pulled out of the resort's lot, he informed us that he was familiar with a lot of people who ventured up into the mountains regularly, so he would introduce us to someone once we got there. I wasn't concerned about being around people we didn't know because we were both genuinely people persons. And no matter where we were or who was around, I always felt safe with Jahsani.

The sky seemed to darken as we began ascending the mountains. I could tell we were getting close because we passed a couple of guys walking on the side of the road in that direction. We suddenly came upon several vehicles parked along the side of the road. Monty pulled over and parked beside an old Honda.

As soon as we got out the van, I saw the dense fog ascending. The cycle of transformation was taking place right before our eyes as the morning dew converted back into gas.

We followed Monty into the darkness of the brush until the low sounds of drumming and chanting, and the familiar scent of marijuana being smoked, got louder and stronger. I could see the glow of a campfire ahead of us.

The trail opened up to an area along the stream. Several men and women stood around talking and smoking. I could see a few others over by the stream meditating. There was also a small group sitting on a fallen tree in front of a burning fire. Three men with long locs were playing the drums and chanting to the rhythm of a slow, bass-thumping riddim.

A short Rasta with big, natty locs down to his waist greeted us.

"Monty. Grand rising, bredren. How have you been?"

"Every ting cool, bredren. Mi got good people from the States who wanted to come pon the mountain to meditate this morning. Dem want the real experience."

"Respect," said the Rasta. He waved over a slim dark-skinned woman who had her locs pinned up in a cute style. "Peace, sistren and bredren. Dem call me Jah Shaka, and this me empress, Sandy."

"Peace. I'm Hanifa, and this is my husband Jahsani."

Jah Shaka smiled. "Aah, da prince," he said, fully aware what Jahsani's name meant. "All are welcome pon da mountain. You can meditate anywhere you like. We were about to load up da ponta if you'd like to join us."

"Sure," I replied, then followed Sandy over to a bench on the left side of the fire.

Sandy grabbed the ponta, which looked like a hookah. She put some ganja on the pipe filter, lit it, and inhaled. There was so much smoke when she exhaled that it looked like a bomb cloud. It was my turn. I inhaled and smoke filled my lungs so fast that I had to fight off choking. It was definitely high-grade herb. Jahsani hit it, then passed it to Jah Shaka.

I was high after the third hit, so I walked over and sat on an unoccupied log near the stream. I took off my shoes and socks and got in a comfortable position. I grounded myself with deep breaths before channeling the ancestors. My meditation was so calming and peaceful that the 45-minute trance felt like it had been two hours.

The frequency around the camp site was magnified by the vibrations of drumming and chanting and the running stream and the surrounding trees. I saw that dawn had emerged when I opened my eyes. Feeling mentally and spiritually rejuvenated, I put my socks and shoes back on and rejoined Jahsani, Monty, and Jah Shaka over by the smoldering campfire.

"How you feel, queen?"

"I feel great."

We took pictures around the smoldering fire. We got some with us hitting the ponta and blowing smoke, as well as some with our new acquaintances. As we were saying goodbye, Sandy handed me a nice-sized bud of ganja as a parting gift.

"You must've read my mind!" I laughed and gave her a hug.

"Safe travels, queen," she said.

It was 7:30am when we returned to the resort. The sun was slowly rising, and a warm breeze was blowing. Because of how much everyone drank last night, I didn't expect anyone to be up so early, so me and Jahsani went and ate breakfast out by the pool.

"Being on the mountain with them was a wonderful experience," I said to Jahsani. I took a few bites of eggs and potatoes. "I know when I tell the girls they missed out they gon' be mad. But, thanks to Sandy, I'll make it right with a lil' pow-wow."

"Can you imagine how peaceful it must be to do that every morning?"

"It has to feel good because I enjoyed it the entire time we were there."

"If this is our anniversary trip, I'm cool with it because I really enjoyed myself."

"You ain't lying... especially last night," I said with a seductive stare. "You was in yo' bag last night, boo! You was hitting every spot, from every angle, in every position."

"That was all you. You know how wild you get when you get lit."

"Tell you what," I said, feeding him a piece of watermelon from my fruit salad, "it's our last day on the island, so how 'bout we do whatever you want to do."

"Sounds good to me."

I ate a piece of honeydew and pineapple. It tasted so sweet. "What you got in mind, baby?"

"I definitely wanna get in the water. And we gotta get a massage on the beach."

"Aight. How 'bout after we go soak in the tub outside, we go get a couple's massage, then we can hit the beach this afternoon. I'm sure by then everyone will be up."

"I'm with it," he replied as he tossed back the last of his orange juice.

Behind the bungalow was a private botanical area with an alfresco claw-foot tub on a wooden slab. It had been a long time since we shared a bath together, so I drew us a nice bubble bath.

Jahsani came out the back door in a robe with two glasses in one hand and a bottle of champagne in the other. The water was nice and hot, and the champagne was ice cold. We sat at opposite ends, relaxing, talking, and drinking. There was a papable sexual charge in the water, and knowing Jahsani the way I did, I could tell by how he was looking at me that he was up to something.

As he refilled our glasses, I gently rubbed my foot against his dick and balls. Within seconds, it was elongated and hard. He sat his glass on the deck, grabbed the soap, and lathered my leg, calf, and foot. I sipped the champagne, growing hornier by the second.

He started kissing my foot. Sensing what was about to go down, I sat my glass to the side and watched as he passionately licked and sucked my toes, one by one, until he reached the big toe. I closed my eyes and rubbed my nipples as the warmth and wetness of his mouth sent a titillating sensation upward from my foot to my pussy and chest.

He switched to the other foot and repeated the same process. He stared at me with loving eyes as he slowly and erotically sucked my toes. He stopped and rolled my leg over, forcing me on all fours. I arched my back, lifting my butt higher in the air. My legs were spread; my pussy was open and heartily inviting him in.

While massaging the globes of my butt, he ran his hand down the crack of my ass and playfully slid a finger all the way in my soapy pussy. After a few strokes, he added a second finger. "Ooh, Jahsani," I delightfully cooed. I looked back at him. He enjoyed watching his fingers go in and out of my pussy, so I pivoted my hips to give his fingers a little workout.

"Stand up, 'Nifa," he ordered, withdrawing his fingers. I stood up, spread my legs, bent over, and held onto the edge of the tub, readying myself for whatever was coming next.

Jahsani spread my cheeks with his strong fingers, then buried his face in my ass and began licking my pussy and rubbing my clit. "Aaaah... baby," I moaned, surprised at the unexpected treat.

The warm breeze from him breathing through his nose tickled my asshole. My body tingled as he flickered his tongue across my clit. "Yes... yes... this yo' pussy, baby," I uttered as the exhilarating sensation of an orgasm reverberated throughout my entire body, causing me to get weak in the knees.

Jahsani realized my legs were unstable, so he pulled me back down on my knees and positioned himself between my legs. He rubbed his dick up and down my wet slit, then inserted it to the hilt. "Ooh, yesss!" I moaned, melting into the sweet sensation. Careful not to stroke too fast and cause the waters to overrun, Jahsani stroked long and slow.

I wanted to feel more pressure, so I pushed against the edge of the tub and forced him to go deeper. He switched his stroke to deep, hip swirls. All four of my walls smiled as he touched them, giving them the attention they so craved. My moans of pleasure grew louder, and his groans grew grittier. I felt another surge coming on. I could no longer remain calm. I began bucking back at him vehemently, causing my titties to sway and water to splash out the tub in the process. "I'm cummin, baby... I'm cummin'."

Jahsani's heavy breathing turned into deep grunts, so I knew he was cummin' also. Once his thrust came to a halt, he pulled out and sat down with his head resting on the edge of the tub. I turned around.

"Uh-un... you know what it is. Stand up," I ordered.

He stood up and I put his dick in my mouth. I began sucking the head. It was so sensitive that he could barely take it. His legs trembled uncontrollably. I slowly sucked his dick, savoring the rivulets that came out of it until it was as limp as a wet noodle. I then bathed him while he remained standing. When I finished, I looked up at him and said, "The royal penis is clean, your highness!"

We burst out laughing together.

The temperature had risen into the upper 70s by 10:30am, so Jahsani and I decided to go get a couple's massage. We had no idea we'd run into Will and Carmen.

"Hey, girl! Where y'all on y'all way to?" I asked.

"To get something to eat. My stomach's touching my back," replied Carmen.

"I already know," I said, remembering how hungry I was when we first got up.

"You look bright-eyed. Where y'all headed?"

"Girl, we been up since 4:30 this morning. We went up on the mountain and meditated. Look," I showed her the pictures on my phone. "We're on our way to get a couple's massage.

Her face lit up with excitement as she scrolled through the pictures. "Y'all was just chillin' with the Rastas, smoking good and kickin' it."

"It was cool. And... I got a lil' som'em som'em for a pow-wow session later."

"Aye, just let me know when and I'm at yo' door!" assured a smiling Carmen. "Aight. Well, if anyone ask, I'll let'em know where y'all at."

"Aight. Later."

There were several people getting massages on the beach, so we had to wait on the next available masseuses. Jahsani's was a tall, dark-skinned woman with braids. Mine was a short, stocky built man with wavy hair. Both were dressed in all white uniforms.

My masseuse drizzled oil on my back, smeared it all over, then began massaging my shoulders. His soft but strong hands went down my spine and lower back, applying pressure for deep tissue compressions. It felt so good that I mentally drifted off for a moment.

As he began massaging the backs of my legs, I subconsciously imagined it was Jahsani squeezing, rubbing, and nudging out my tightness. The masseuse slowly worked his way up my hamstring and inner thigh. I thought about how good Jahsani ate my pussy from the back and fucked me afterwards. The closer the masseuse's hands got to my goodies, the wetter I got. It felt so surreal that as he squeezed my inner thigh, I let out an orgasmic moan. "Mmmm."

The sound of Jahsani's voice brought me out of my reverie.

"It feels that good, baby?"

My response was an all out moan. "Yes!"

Had our session lasted two more minutes, I would have came in my bathing suit.

We thanked them for the amazing massages and headed to the main dining hall to get a fruit salad. Everyone finally surfaced and was sitting on the patio enjoying breakfast. We walked over to join them.

"Hey, everybody!" I greeted as I sat down.

"Hey, you!" replied Brooke. "I heard y'all went up on the mountain this morning," she said with a playfully jealous and upset stare.

"Don't be mad. After the way we celebrated last night, I didn't think anyone wanted to be woke up at 4:30." I handed her my phone so she could see the pictures. "I met a cool sister up there named Sandy, and she blessed me with a lil' som'em som'em, so when y'all get a minute, come through for a pow-wow."

I could tell from Brooke's facial expressions as she looked over the pics that she wished she had experienced the mountain, too. "Michaela commented on the picture of us with five Rastas by the smoldering fire. "Were you scared being up there with them?"

"Not at all. They were nice and welcoming. We took part in their sacrament of smoking ganja out of the ponta you see me holding."

"A ponta?" Michaela repeated. "That looks like a hookah to me."

"Same thing, different name. Y'all know I'm a Cali girl. I done smoked out of bongs, bowls, and face masks... but that ponta hit hard! My first hit, I thought my lungs was gon' bust."

Jahsani's eyes shimmered with excitement as he spoke. "The way them brothers beat on them drums and chanted was like some shit you only see in the movies! You would've had to been there to appreciate the vibe."

By the looks of Michaela's hair, I could tell their night was an eventful one. "How you feeling this morning, Mrs. I's Engaged Now?" I teased in my The Color Purple voice.

Smiling from ear to ear, Michaela held out her left hand, showing off her beautiful diamond ring. "High! Shocked! I'm still wrapping my mind around everything."

"Well, I'm glad I was here to witness that moment for you. It's the highlight of the trip," I assured her.

"Stop before you make me cry again." She fanned her eyes. "Thanks, 'Nifa."

Michaela gathered herself and then addressed the group. "It's our last day here. Do y'all want to enjoy the day with y'all's boo, or kick it together?"

"I'm going to spend the day with Jahsani. He wants to go back on the beach, so that's where we'll be. However, our driver told us about a spot called Blackwell's Rum Bar, so we're going to watch the sunset and have a few cocktails if anyone wants to join us."

The idea of watching the sunset appealed to everyone's romantic side. They all agreed to go have cocktails with us later. With that understood, I told the girls to come to my bungalow at 6pm for a pow-wow.

It was another beautiful day in paradise. Jahsani and I went snorkeling down by the rock coral. We went jet skiing once more and then got drinks and relaxed in the chaise lounge on the beach under an umbrella.

For as far as my eyes could see, there was nothing but clear blue skies and ocean in view. The thought of our fairytale weekend coming to an end and returning to our normal lives was beginning to sink in. I reached over and held Jahsani's hand.

"I'm so glad we came, baby. We needed this vacation," I said, looking at him as he sipped his drink.

"You must've felt my energy because I was just thinking the same thing. Enjoying time with you has made me realize how consumed we are running our businesses that we unintentionally neglect each other."

"It's not that I don't want to spend more time with you, baby. But after working all day, I come home and help the kids with their school work, start dinner, clean up, and by the time you get home I'm exhausted."

"I know, baby. The fact of the matter is your time is split between me and the kids, with more emphasis on them right now, and rightfully so. I'll never complain because you do your best to keep everything together, and I appreciate you. It's been ten beautiful years, and the next ten will be even better." He leaned over and kissed me.

At 6pm, the girls convened at my bungalow while the fellas went and shot pool at the sports bar. We sat on the sofas in front of the open sliding door. I rolled two joints while Michaela poured everyone a glass of champagne. Brooke lit the first joint and passed it to Carmen.

"This remind me of how we used to kick it back in our dorm room days," said Brooke.

Michaela's face lit up with excitement. "Remember that time we was smoking and the hall monitor was going door to door trying to figure out where the weed smell was coming from. We panicked and was scrambling around opening windows, trying to fan the smoke out before she got to our door, and Carmen's crazy ass was spraying lemon Pledge in the air... like that shit was gon' make a difference!"

We all laughed.

I hit the joint and passed it to Michaela. "What y'all do today?" I asked.

"Me and Carl went rafting down the Rio Grande on a bamboo raft. The scenery and water was so tranquil and beautiful," said Michaela. She passed her phone around so we could see the pictures and video she shot.

"Seven and I visited an old sugar cane plantation that once held kidnapped Africans waiting to be transported to the Americas. We walked the grounds, saw the small shacks the slaves lived in, and other historical artifacts." Brooke passed her phone around to show us the pictures.

"What about you, Carmen?" I asked as she fired up the second joint.

"Girl, me and Will's greedy ass went back to Claudia's and ate some of that good food!" she answered in such a way that we all laughed. "We just been enjoying our last day here, relaxing together, because I got four tyrants waiting to get on my nerves as soon as we get back to Atlanta." She passed the joint to me.

"I feel you. Me and Jahsani been doing the same thing. We took a bath outside together, got a couple's massage, jet skied, snorkeled, then chilled on the beach."

"What didn't y'all do?" teased Brooke.

"Aye, I'm just thankful we got to spend some time together," I smiled.

"Damn!" shouted Carmen. "Is it me, or is that some good ass weed? I'm high as shit!"

"Nah, it's fyah!" Michaela answered as she took the last hit and stubbed it out in the ashtray.

With our eyes low and feeling super-mellow, we washed our hands, tidied up, put on our sunglasses to mask our high eyes, then headed out to get the guys.

We found them at the sports bar. They were having drinks and in the middle of laughing about something when I wrapped my arms around Jahsani's neck and kissed him.

"What y'all laughing at?" I asked.

Trying to stop laughing, he answered, "Nothing!"

Someone had clearly shared something they didn't want us to know, and he was honoring the guy code. He wrapped his arms around the small of my back.

"Y'all ready?" I asked.

"I've been ready for you my whole life," he flirtatiously responded.

Without further delay, we walked outside where Monty was waiting in front of the van. Everyone boarded and took a seat. Monty pulled off.

The van was filled with conversation, laughter, and stories about our individual experiences the entire time Monty drove to the west side of the island. Monty pointed out landmarks that were used in movies, and the exotic villas that stars and entertainers vacationed at.

we finally pulled up at Blackwell's Rum Bar, a reddish-brown cave along the mountainside. The sounds of a live band playing instrumentals could be heard as soon as we stepped out of the van.

Will held the door open while we walked inside. There was a small crowd sitting around, so we made our way toward the sounds of music on the patio. The crowd out there was larger. People were playing volleyball on the side, some were listening to the band, and others were just hanging out and having a good time. This is where the action was.

The view of the crystal-clear, blue ocean and adjacent rock cliff reminded me of a villain's lair in a movie. Blackwell's was known for its Campari cocktails, so we decided to try it. Carl bought the first round. I instantly understood why this was the drink they were known for after my first sip. It was the best on the island.

Will got our attention. "Aye, check this out." He was pointing at the adjacent cliff where several guys were about to jump in the ocean. We walked over to the patio's edge to get a better view.

There were two shirtless, dark-skinned guys wearing trunks, and one white guy who was dressed like he might have been at Blackwell's having drinks before we arrived. A guy with short hair leaped off the 35-foot cliff and did a swan dive into the water below. The crowd that had gathered on the terrace whistled and applauded like it was a competition. They cheered again when the second guy leaped off the cliff and did a double somersault into the water.

As the white guy inched his way closer to the edge of the cliff, a group of men and women cheered and egged him on. They seemed drunk. I'm sure their friend was, too. The suspense of an average Joe jumping from a 35-foot cliff grew as he looked over the edge. And, then, he suddenly jumped and plunged feet first into the water. His courage caused the terrace crowd to erupt with cheers.

We found an empty sitting area near the corner of the terrace, so we posted up right there to enjoy the view. The sun was getting closer to the horizon, and the color of the sky transitioned from a calm blue to a Starburst orange and, finally, to a pinkish-purplish hue. It was so beautiful that everyone on the terrace was in awe.

People began taking pictures with the sunset in the background. Great idea! Always take advantage of nature's beauty. I took one with Jahsani standing behind me, his arms wrapped around my body.

Darkness settled in by the third round of Camparis. The vibe was mellow. Everyone was enjoying themselves. Michaela stood up to say something.

"I just wanna say thank you for coming to celebrate my fiancé's birthday with us," she smilingly said. "This has been the best vacation I've ever had, and I hope we plan another one together next summer." She sat down on Carl's thigh.

"I agree," added Brooke. "This has been an amazing trip, and I'm looking forward to y'all's wedding!"

"That part!" championed Carmen.

The crowd was thinning out, so we decided to head back to the resort. We got there around 9pm. The night was still young. The others wanted to go hang out at the sports bar, but me and Jahsani wanted to enjoy our last hours in paradise alone, so we broke from the group and took a romantic stroll along the beach.

We talked and watched the tide wash ashore. We sat in the sand and stared out at the ocean. Ever since our conversation earlier, something heavy had been on my mind. I figured now was a good time to bring it up.

"Can I ask you something?"

"Always, baby," he replied.

"Earlier, you said a lot has changed over our ten years together, and I agree with that. But what do you anticipate will change in the next ten years?" He stared out into the darkness of the night. I could tell he was giving my question some serious thought.

"In the next ten years, the dynamics of our family will evolve. The kids will be older, start driving, become more independent, and require less of our time. There's the possibility of college or pursuing whatever dreams they may have. The demands of life will change, hell, our love and relationship will change."

That's what was troubling me. "Why do you think our love and relationship will change?"

"It has to. Change isn't necessarily a bad thing. It's just the process of evolution. Our love will grow stronger than it is now. We'll be mor experienced in areas we were once naïve. We must change in order to grow together, baby," he explained. "Don't worry, I ain't going nowhere. As long as we got each other, we're growing old together."

"Promise?"

"I put that on everything I love."

I leaned over and kissed him, but the look in his eyes pulled me in for more. Our tongues engaged in passionate exchanges, triggering the enactment of my sexual fantasy of making love on the beach under the moonlight and stars.

No one was on the beach, so I straddled his lap and unbuckled his belt and shorts button. Having on a t-shirt dress and no panties allowed things to unfold quite easily. He pulled his shorts down, and without either of us using our hands, his dick pressed against my wet slit and slid inside of me like my pussy had a home beacon device attached to it.

The length of his dick gliding in and out sent currents of bliss coursing through my body. The sensation felt even better once the reality of fulfilling another fantasy registered in my mind. I rocked back and forth like I was dancing to music only I could hear. He squeezed my butt then retracted to the tip of his flanged head before explosively thrusting up into me, jolting my body.

"Uaahh! Baby, do it again," I requested in a low moan as I felt the beginnings of an orgasm building. He caressed my butt, spread my cheeks, retracted to the tip, and explosively thrusted and jolted my body once more. "Yesss! Again!" I demanded, pressing against his chest to brace myself. He did it again and again. With each stroke, I made weird noises as we simultaneously came.

Ooum...

Oum...

Oum, oum, oum!!!

When Jahsani finally stopped impaling me, neither of us moved. There was an overwhelming euphoria of ecstasy flowing between us. We laid there for several minutes, listening to the tide and enjoying the memory we just created.

Chapter 13

(Brooke)

Two weeks after returning from Jamaica, my relationship with Seven blossomed tremendously. He came over and spent more time with me and Yasmin. He would play and read books with her. He would sometimes cook and spend the night. It felt good falling asleep in the warmth of his arms and waking up to multiple orgasms. To walk in the bathroom and see his toothbrush and shower bag on the counter filled my heart with joy because it was proof we were moving forward.

My morning workouts with Michaela would soon come to an end as the upcoming school year was just a few weeks away. Part of me was ready to return and be with my students, the other part didn't want summer to end so soon.

Today's workout was intense and energy draining. We had 15 minutes left on the elliptical when I began feeling lightheaded. I got off the machine and sat on the bench to drink some water. Michaela gave me a concerned look.

Still on the elliptical, she asked, "Are you aight, Brooke?"

"Yeah. I just got a little lightheaded."

"Did you eat anything this morning?"

"Just a banana on the way out."

"You know you gotta put fuel in the body before and after each workout."

"The only fuel my body been running on is Seven," I joked as I tried to catch my breath.

"I know that's right! How does it feel with him being there more?"

"We love it. Yas has someone to play with her, and for me it's amazing," I smiled.

"I told y'all... that morning dick hit different, don't it?"

I nodded my head in agreement. "Have y'all thought about a date, yet?"

She was going into cool down mode. "Not yet. He wants to wait to see what's going on with the house before taking that on, too."

"That makes sense."

After Michaela's cool down, we grabbed our things and went to the Juice Bar. We replenished our bodies and went our separate ways. I went home and ate a chicken wrap. I then took a hot shower and took a quick nap.

Two hours later, the sound of my phone ringing woke me up. It was Seven. I answered in a slumberous tone.

"Hey, bae."

"Good afternoon, beautiful. Were you sleeping?"

"Just napping before I have to go get Yas."

"You sound tired, baby. I'll go pick her up for you if you wanna rest."

His offer sounded good, but he didn't have a car seat in his truck. "That's okay. I'm about to get up and grab something to eat on the way to get her. How's your day going?"

"Peaceful. Just got confirmation from the last artist who is sending his work down next week for the showcase, so I'm feeling pretty good, especially now that I've heard your voice."

"Do you have anything special planned for the showing?"

"Yeah! It's gonna be dope, too. Make sure your girls know it's next week."

"Okay. Are you coming over tonight?"

"Of course! It's TACO TUESDAY!" he shouted. "I'm gon' cook for y'all."

"Aye, works for me."

"I'll be there around five-thirty. Any special requests regarding wine?"

"Moscato, please."

"Gotchu. See you later, beautiful."

"Peace."

Communication with Darius continued to be cordial, but I could tell he had an open wound from seeing me with Seven. Darius and I agreed he would pick up Yasmin on Fridays so they could have two days together instead of one. It was their weekend together, so as soon as I got home from the gym I took a shower and prepared her bag.

Seven and I had been planning a romantic dinner for the past week. I was looking forward to the weekend stay-cation at his place. With Yasmin down for a nap, I started getting myself together. I tied my locs up, put on a sexy, green, laced panty and bra set, an olive-green, denim shirt-dress, and the hemp-wedge sandals I bought in Jamaica.

Darius arrived at 5:30pm. I opened the door and saw him dressed in a nice, navy-blue suit. He always did have a good taste in fashion.

"You look nice," I said, letting him in.

"Thanks. So do you."

When I handed him Yasmin's bag, he noticed I had one of my own sitting at the bottom of the stairs.

"Looks like you're going somewhere."

"I am," I replied.

"Will I be able to reach you in case of an emergency?"

"All you gotta do is call my phone," I nonchalantly responded. I then opened the door so I could put Yasmin's car seat in his car.

Entertaining Darius's prying attempts was something I'd learned to avoid like pot holes in the street. Besides, I had a hot dinner date waiting on me. Yes! Mr. Wonderful was waiting on me.

I was on a first name basis with the garage attendants at Seven's building, so Byron raised the rail when he saw me pull up.

"How you doing, Byron?"

"Same shit, different day. I'll let'em know you're on your way up."

"Thanks. Have a good evening."

When the elevator doors opened, Seven was standing there dressed in all black with a bouquet of roses. The top two buttons on his shirt were unbuttoned, and he looked like a model on the cover of GQ Magazine.

"Let me get that bag for you," he said, exchanging the flowers for my bag.

"You look handsome," I commented with a lustful smile.

"Thanks. You look gorgeous as always." He headed to the back with my bag.

Aaliyah's song *One in a Million* was playing through the speakers, and something in the kitchen was smelling amazingly delicious. Not only was Seven sexy, smart, and could cook, he had great taste in music as well.

"Dinner's almost ready. Would you like a glass of wine or something else?" he asked upon entering the room.

"Wine, please," I answered, staring at the beautiful view of the city.

"Coming right up."

The dining table was set up for two with a burning candle placed in the middle of it. It was obvious he put a lot of effort and thought into the evening. He handed me a glass of wine.

"So, what's for dinner tonight, Chef Sexy?"

"Crab cakes with hollandaise sauce, broccoli, and my grandma's special mac and cheese," he answered with a cocky attitude like he knew his family recipe was the bomb.

I took a sip of wine. "I hope you didn't defame her recipe."

"What? Blasphemy!" he responded, smiling. "Have I disappointed you yet?"

"You're right. I'm just saying, not everyone's mac and cheese be poppn'. Now, I would never say your grandma's mac and cheese is trash, but who's to say yours taste like hers?" I asked, giving him a questionable stare.

"Ooh... you just disrespectful today. It's all good because I promise I'm gon' make you eat those words."

He opened the oven to check the mac and cheese. He pulled it out and sat it on top of the stove to let it cool down.

"Come try one of these," he said, holding a tray of smoked oysters.

I turned my face up because I wasn't a big fan of oysters.

"Just try one," he prodded, then sucked one down.

My face lit up at the sound of him slurping a second oyster down. It reminded me of the sound he makes when eating my pussy.

"You like the sound of that, huh?" He smiled then slurped another one down.

I grabbed one off the tray and shucked it down. Surprisingly, it wasn't as bad as I remembered oysters being, so I took another one.

"See, I told you they're good."

"I see you on yo' aphrodisiac vibe tonight," I teased.

"It goes with the theme of the evening," he laughed.

He plated the food and brought it to the table. The crab cakes had a light drizzle of hollandaise sauce on them. The broccoli looked firm. The mac and cheese was golden with a few burned spots on top, just like someone's grandma had made it. He took a sip of wine and stared at me.

"I guess you waiting on me to try yo' mac and cheese, huh?" I asked, blushing.

"You already know."

I put my fork in and retrieved a bite full. The cheese stretched until it finally gave way. I put it in my mouth. It was good, so I got more. The taste exploded in my mouth after a few bites. I turned away so he couldn't see my facial expression of utter satisfaction. He burst out laughing.

"Talk to me, I talk back," he confidently stated.

Forced to admit my wrong, I nodded my head, giving him props. "This mac and cheese is the bomb. You did your grandma's recipe justice."

"I'm glad it gets your stamp of approval. But, if I tell you a duck can pull a truck, believe me! Now let's eat."

"I hear you. I just got one question. What's in it that's giving it that extra umph?"

He looked at me with a huge smile on his face. "In due time, my luv."

Throughout dinner, we talked about the upcoming school year, next week's art showcase, and our weekly experiences. His ability to carry on a conversation about anything was truly his best quality.

After the wonderful dinner, we refilled our glasses and chilled on the sofa that faced the view of the city. The buzz from the wine kicked in as the sound of Toni Tone Tony's *It Never Rains in Southern California* further set the mood.

"Thank you for the excellent dinner, babe," I said, running my finger through his locs.

"You're welcome. I can tell you enjoyed it because you smashed two servings tonight."

"I was hungry," I playfully justified. "I saved my appetite all day so I could enjoy your dinner."

"It's all good. I love cooking for you, baby." He kissed my arm. "Just like I love making you smile, making you happy, and making you moan in pleasure."

The sound of his voice was turning me on. "And I love that you do all of those things for me, baby." I kissed his head.

"Have you given any thought to our conversation on the beach?"

"It's crossed my mind a time or two since we've been back."

"And?"

"I'm still thinking things through."

"I said I wouldn't pressure you, and I won't. It's just that I love falling asleep with you in my arms and waking up to your pretty smile in the morning." He paused. "Take all the time you need, baby."

It sounded like he felt rejected, so I sat my glass on the table to clarify things. "I'm not saying no, Seven. I just don't want it to seem rushed or too soon."

"I get where you coming from. Personally, I don't care what others may think, but I do care about how you feel, so whenever you're ready to take that next step, let me know."

The intro to Janet Jackson's *Any Time, Any Place* came on. "This my jam!" I excitedly exclaimed.

He grabbed the remote and turned it up as I prepared myself to sing along.

In the thundering rain... stare into my eyes

I can feel your hands moving up my thighs

Skirt around my waist, wall against my face

I can feel your lips...

Seven stood up and held his hand out for mine. "Dance with me," he said. Flattered, I gave him my hand and he helped me up. I wrapped my hands behind his neck as he pressed his body against mine, and we began to sensually slow dance. I resumed singing while he caressed my back and my butt.

As I recited the lyrics to the song, I felt the power of their true meaning and realized I was allowing fear of the past and what others might think prevent me from doing what I really wanted to do, which was to be with Seven... to be happy.

The scent of his cologne, his smooth rhythm, and the sensual vibe had my juices pooling in my panties. I looked at him with loving eyes. "Yes." That's all I said. Understanding exactly what was meant by that one word, Seven passionately kissed me. We kissed and danced in sync with the seductive bassline for the remainder of the song. He broke off our kiss, leaving me wanting more.

"I have a surprise for you," he said, then led me by the hand down the hall to the closed bedroom door. I opened the door and a sweltering sensation overcame me. The room was filled with burning candles of different sizes. Rose petals were scattered over the floor, leading to the bed, which they also covered.

No one had ever gone to such lengths to woo me. I began unbuttoning the remaining buttons on my shirt-dress and let it fall to the floor, exposing my sexy lingerie set. I then turned my attention to him.

I unbuttoned the rest of his shirt, then his pants. My mouth watered at the protrusion in his silk boxers. I dropped to both knees as I pulled them down. The flickering of the candle's flames made his big, black dick look even bigger than usual. I ran the flat of my tongue up the shaft to the tip, swirled it around the mushroom-shaped head, then took it into my wet mouth several times.

He towered above me in a kingly manner, enjoying the treatment he was truly worthy of. I looked up at his imposing figure and placed my hands on his hips. I let him fuck my mouth while I moaned and sucked profusely. "Ooh, yeah! Get it, baby," he blissfully uttered as he securely held the back of my head. I sucked, slurped, and deep throated his dick until I started to feel dizzy.

Slowly, I raised up and stood on my two feet. I removed my bra and panties and laid in the bed. He crawled between my legs and planted a series of kisses on my body. He moved from my neck to my breasts around my areola, then pinched my nipples with his supple lips.

Seven wasn't just another guy with a big dick; he was a skillful lover. He kissed down my body, spreading my legs further apart as he moved. He parted my pussy lips with his thumbs and licked up and down, side to side, and all around. He then inserted his tongue as far as it would go. I melted in ecstasy. "Aah! Ooh, baby," I moaned, caressing his head with both hands.

He pushed the hood back, exposing my clit, which he began licking, slurping, and suckling. My back arched off the bed as the electrifying sensation felt like a million volts of charged pleasure streaming through my body at one time. "Oooohhh!" I screamed, locking his head between my thighs as they shuddered and shook for several seconds.

"Oh, my God! Oh, my God!" I heavily panted.

"Relax, baby," he mumbled.

How could I relax when the feeling was so exhilarating? I slowly eased my legs back open so he could continue.

He licked the outer edges of my pussy, then stuck his middle finger inside of me and massaged my g-spot while flickering his tongue on my clit. I tried to wriggle away but I couldn't. He was locked on it like a pitbull on a bone.

"Seven! Babyyyy! Pleeeaase!" I begged for mercy as the powerful sensation of an orgasm rippled all over my body.

By the grace of God, he relented. He retracted his tongue and withdrew his finger. I was breathing so heavy I couldn't catch my breath. He kissed up my body and started sucking on my nipples again. This allowed me to calm my breathing.

I felt him enter me. The pleasurable sensation of pressure caused me to let out a deep moan. "Uuaahhhh!" He started off with shallow strokes but gradually built up to deep thrusts that made me have subsequent orgasms every three minutes. I don't know how he does it, but it was the second time he took me there.

And then he did something new. He sat back on his knees and placed my left leg on his left shoulder. This created an angle that allowed him to hit spots I didn't even know were my spots. As he watched my eyes roll into the back of my head with each stroke, my moans of pleasure filled the room.

"You like that, baby?" he asked, slowing the pace.

"I love it."

"How much you love it?"

"So much that I'm cummin' on it again right now." I closed my eyes and gyrated on his dick.

"Right now?" he repeated, picking up the pace.

"Right now... ooh, baby! Aaaahhh!"

"Uuuuuaaah!" he groaned as he exploded inside of me and collapsed.

I wrapped my arms around his body and we lay there breathing heavily. Within 15, our breathing synchronized and we fell asleep.

I was awakened by a nauseating feeling. I got up to use the bathroom but ended up vomiting instead. I figured it was from the oysters last night. I urinated and washed my hands. I went back into the bedroom and, to my surprise, there was a note attached to the clock on the nightstand that read: *I gotta run to the gallery to accept a delivery. I'll be back by 1pm.* It was 11:30am.

I was brushing my teeth when I heard my phone ringing. It was in the living room, so I scampered to get it.

I answered in an odd tone, "Hello?"

"We got the house!" shouted Michaela.

I rinsed my mouth in the kitchen sink.

"Hellooo!" said Michaela. "Did you hear me, Brooke?"

"Yeah. Congratulations," I casually responded.

"Are you aight?"

"Yeah. Seven cooked some oysters last night and they must've upset my stomach 'cause I went to use the bathroom but threw up. I was brushing my teeth when I answered the phone."

"Um hmm... are you sure you're not pregnant?"

"Quit playing, Michaela." I changed the subject. "When do y'all close on the house?"

"We close Saturday."

"That's what's up. Let me know when you having the house warming."

"Oh, y'all gon' know when we moving, too, so y'all can help," she kidded. "Aight, girl. I just had to call someone and shout. Hit me up later."

"Aight. Peace."

Michaela's remark got me thinking long and hard about the possibility of being pregnant. *We don't use protection. I'm not on birth control. I've been sleeping and eating more than usual, and having dizzy spells.* I rubbed my forehead, trying to convince myself it was just the oysters that upset my stomach. There was only one way to be for sure, and that was to take a test.

I washed my face, threw on some leggings and a t-shirt, and drove around the corner to CVS to pick up a test. I went back to Seven's and took it. After doing so, I sat nervously on the toilet waiting for the results. Minutes later, a positive sign showed on the stick. I dropped my head in disbelief.

My mind immediately began running in a million and one directions. *How am I going to tell Seven? What will be his reaction? How will it affect our relationship?* I dreaded calling and letting my parents know I was pregnant.

I needed to calm my thoughts. I got off the toilet, undressed, and hopped in the shower. As the hot water rained down on me, I rubbed my stomach, knowing that life was in the early stages of forming inside of me. I was unsure if I should be happy or sad, but I was certain I'd have the baby. I decided to tell Seven when he returned home.

After I got out the shower and got myself together, I put on some black leggings and a t-shirt, then proceeded to straightening up the room. I was sitting on the terrace in deep thought when the sound of my name being called snapped me out of it. "Out here!" I shouted to Seven.

He stepped out on the terrace wearing basketball shorts, a Nike 'Just Do It' t-shirt, and retro Jordans. "What's up, queen?" He seemed excited to see me. He kissed me and sat down beside me.

"How are things at the gallery?"

"Good. Everything's ready to be hung and exhibited."

"That's good," I said while staring out at the city's view.

"What's wrong, baby? You look like something's on your mind."

I took a deep breath to calm my nerves. "Do you love me?" I asked as tears welled up in my eyes.

"Of course I love you. What's going on, Brooke?"

Fighting back the tears, I pulled the EPT stick out my waistband and handed it to him.

"What's this?" he asked before looking at it. After seeing what it was, he looked at me. "Is this what I think it is?"

I nodded my head, waiting to see his reaction.

He stood up and looked at the city view, then turned around with the biggest smile ever. "Come here, baby!"

He helped me to my feet, then picked me up in a joyous hug. His warm embrace erased all the doubts I thought of earlier. I wrapped my arms around his neck and partook in his happiness. He kissed me and started talking really fast.

"If it's a boy, let's name him after me. If it's a girl, we can name her Brooklyn."

"Slow down, speedy," I jested. "I just took the test, so I gotta go to the doctor and find out how far along I am."

He was overly excited. "Right, right. Okay, uh... when will you know for sure?"

"I called my doctor and made an appointment for Monday morning."

"Aight. I'll take you, if that's okay with you?"

"That'll be fine."

Seeing how excited he was excited me. He knelt down, kissed my stomach, then rested his face on it.

Seven drove me to the doctor's appointment Monday morning. As the doctor performed the examination and took blood, he sat quietly in the corner of the room and paid attention to everything. I was three weeks pregnant; my due date was May 9th, a month after his birthday.

As soon as we got in the truck, I called and told my mother the good news. She was happy for us. She assured me that her and my father would come stay with us when it was time for the baby to be born.

Seven and I stopped and ate breakfast at Jackie's. He then dropped me off at home so he could go make sure the setup for the showcase was going as planned.

It was time to share the good news with my sisters, so I put them on a group call. Hanifa answered on the first ring.

"Good morning, lady."

"Hey, 'Nifa. Hold on." I merged the calls.

"What's up, Brooke?" asked Michaela.

"Hanifa's on the line, too."

"Hi, 'Nifa," greeted Michaela.

"What's going on, busy woman? When are y'all getting the keys to the house?" inquired Hanifa.

"Saturday!" answered an excited Michaela.

They had high-jacked the call and acted like I wasn't the one who called them, so I abruptly interrupted their conversation. "Utt-umm!" I loudly cleared my throat.

"My bad, principal meany," teased Hanifa. "What's up, Brooke?"

"Thank you very much. I was calling to remind you ladies that

Seven's Black Love showcase is Thursday at 7pm."

"I wouldn't miss it for the world," claimed Hanifa. "There might be something I can buy for the house and spa with that theme."

"Michaela, could you do a promo blitz on your blog to increase awareness of the event?" I asked.

"Listen at you, promoting yo' man like you the Michelle Obama of the art gallery! I got you, sis."

The three of us got a good laugh at that one.

"Oh, and before I forget, come May, you two will be aunties again."

"Aunties? Again?" Hanifa repeated. "You pregnant?"

"I knew it!" shouted Michaela. "And yo' ass talking 'bout some oysters made you throw up. Anyway, congratulations, Brooke!"

Thank you."

"How did Seven react when you told him?" asked Hanifa.

"He was ecstatic! He started thinking of names like I was in labor. I was like, 'slow down, speedy.'"

"This will be his first child, right?" asked Michaela.

"Yeah."

"How does Yas feel about being a big sister?"

"Yas just want someone to boss around," I answered. "What's the deal on y'all's anniversary?"

"Since it's going to be the end of the summer, we're going to hire an event planner and have a cookout at the house, invite our family and friends, and celebrate it like that," said Hanifa.

"That's what's up. Let me know if you need help with anything."

"I'm glad you in a helping mood," Michaela chimed in, "'cause I need help packing my place."

"Okay. Well, ladies, thank you. I love you, and I will holla at y'all later."

"Bye, Brooke. Bye, Michaela."

"Love y'all," said Michaela, ending the call.

Thursday morning was rough on me. My head hurt, and I had been throwing up all night. Seven got out the bed and came to the bathroom door to check on me.

"Are you aight, baby?"

"I'll be okay."

"Do you need anything?"

"Will you bring me some tea, please?"

"Sure."

He headed downstairs and returned five minutes later with hot tea. He sat it on the nightstand beside me, then got back into bed and laid his face on my stomach. This became his thing. The silence was broken by his voice.

"I remember my grandfather telling me the only thing more sacred than a woman's heart is a woman's womb. He said, 'heaven ain't some imaginary place in the sky; heaven is between the legs of a black woman. I understood what he meant by that when I got older."

"What did he mean?" I asked, stroking his head.

"Our African ancestors knew and taught that a woman's womb is the portal for the masculine and feminine principles of the Creative Force to create her/himself in physical form in order to have a human experience. See, your umbilical cord is the gateway that connects the spiritual realm and the physical realm. The first human to manifest was a black woman, and from her womb came all other races of people."

His cultural explanation resonated deep within my spirit and caused a tear to fall from my eye. His love and reverence of our African culture and rituals was so damn sexy.

Today was the art showcase. Seven left around noon to go make a final walk through and get ready. I had a two o'clock loc appointment with the loc-technician at Carmen's salon, so I got up and made Yas and I something to eat, then put some clothes on her and headed to Mrs. Patterson's to drop her off.

Bridgette, the loc-technician, was waiting on me when I entered the salon. I looked toward Carmen's station and saw she was pressing a client's hair.

"Hi, Carmen," I said on my way to Bridgette's chair.

"Hey, momma. You glowin', girl!" she smiled.

"Are y'all coming to the art showcase tonight?"

"Nah. That ain't my scene, plus I'm taking the kids to their cousin's birthday party when I leave here."

"Okay. Maybe you'll check out the next one."

"Michaela said the last one was real nice. I'll think about it."

r Bridgette washed my locs, then I sat under the dryer for a few minutes. Afterwards, she oiled my scalp, palm-rolled my locs, then barrel-rolled them into a super-cute updo. I loved it. I paid her and said goodbye to Carmen on my way out.

On my way home, I swung by the nail salon to get a manicure and pedicure. It was a spur of the moment decision that would leave me pressed for time. After thinking about it inside the shop, I settled for getting French tips only.

My phone started ringing as soon as I stepped in the house. It was Seven.

"Hey, babe," I answered while going up the steps.

"How you feeling?"

"I'm good. Just got in from getting my hair and nails done. About to get in the shower. How are you?"

"I'm good. Everything is set, and people should be arriving in forty-five minutes."

"Okay. See you when I get there. Love you."

"Love you, too, baby."

Seeing as how this might be the last event I attended with my body being my own, I decided to wear my green, body con dress with exposed midriff, and my black, Alexander McQueen sandals with the matching clutch. I laid the dress on the bed and went and hopped in the shower.

While driving down Peachtree, I noticed a lot of cars in the parking lots, and people dressed in upscale attire walking in the direction of the gallery. Thankfully, Seven had told me to pull around the alley behind the gallery and park by the loading dock. There were a few vehicles parked there when I pulled in. the security guard who worked the back let me in the rear door.

I entered the gallery and was immediately blown away by the size of the crowd. There were twice as many people as the last event. The usual attendees were on hand; however, I also noticed younger business-oriented people, cultural savants, professional athletes, and scores of black women. A DJ was on the stage playing neo-soul music, which I found befitting of the theme.

In times past, I looked for Hanifa's afro or Jahsani's locs when trying to spot the girls in the crowd. This night was different. Afros and locs were the chosen hairstyles of the majority. I had no choice but to call Michaela's phone. She answered on the second ring.

"Where you at" she asked.

"I just walked in. Where y'all at? I'm looking around for y'all."

"Over by the photo exhibits."

"I'm heading that way."

There were four exhibits: photos, which consisted of black and white prints; paintings; sculptures; and cultural artifacts.

I spotted Carl and Michaela looking at a photo.

"Hey, you two!" I greeted them both with hugs.

"Your hair's cute, Brooke!" Michaela complimented.

"Thanks." I hugged Hanifa and Jahsani. "Y'all looking good tonight. Their color coordinated outfits were cute.

Sipping on a glass of white wine, Michaela commented, "Girl! It's packed in here like Magic City Mondays at the strip club!"

"You ain't lying. Black Love done brought the city out!" Hanifa agreed.

"What y'all looking at?" I asked. I wondered what the photo was they had been eyeing.

It was a photo of a three to four-year-old black boy and girl sitting on the steps of a brownstone. They were sharing an ice cream cone. It was so adorable.

We stepped over to the next photo, which was of an elderly couple dancing together. Judging them by their fragile bodies, you could tell they had seen and experienced a whole lot over the years. Yet they still looked happy.

The next photo was of profound implications. It was a split picture from the late 1700s that showed two slaves getting married. The other was the wedding ceremony of a free couple from the Bamako people in Gambia. The similarities were astonishing.

We made it over to the paintings exhibit. The first one we saw was so beautiful. It was` of a black man and woman standing in waist deep water at night. The man was holding an infant in the air toward the stars and moon with an inscription that read: *Behold, the only thing greater than you*. I didn't know if it was because I was pregnant and emotionally vulnerable, or if it was what Seven told me that morning about heaven, but the painting moved me. *This would be the perfect gift for Seven,* I thought. Unfortunately, the tag on it said it was SOLD.

The next four paintings were of a series entitled 'Of Earth & Sky'. Each painting held a symbolic meaning for those who understood. The first was of a black woman's face with a hematite stone headdress, symbolizing the ability to absorb energy and to create. The next painting was of a black woman in starry space; it symbolized her ability to bring into existence other life forms, which is a composite of all the elements in the celestial realm.

The third painting was a black woman's face with natural crystals as her headdress. This symbolized her ability to heal, cleanse, and recharge others. Onto the fourth painting; it was simply captivating and caught mine and Hanifa's attention. It was of a posing, sexy, black woman in space inside of a nebula in the constellation of Aries. It symbolized the metaphysical essence of energy and cosmic DNA coming together in the act of creation.

I was enjoying the artwork when Seven suddenly appeared. He wore a black and gold dashiki, black slacks, and loafers.

He greeted us as a group. "What's up, beautiful people?" He singled me out for a personal greeting. "Hey, baby!" Then he kissed me. "How y'all like it?"

Michaela couldn't wait to speak. "Seven, this is dope!"

"The people seem to like it."

Hanifa motioned to the paintings. "Whoever painted these are truly talented and conscious. How much are they?"

"She's a sister from New Jersey, and she's here tonight. If I see her, I'll introduce you to her. As far as price, the paintings are $2000 apiece and can be bought individually."

"Is that a good price?" she asked.

"Actually, it is. These are one of ones, so if you're interested you might wanna act now 'cause folks are buying up things fast."

"I see," I commented. "I was gonna buy you that first painting of the man holding up the infant, but it's already sold."

Seven smiled and winked at me, indicating he was the buyer. "Tell you what, Hanifa. Y'all family, so if you want two paintings, I'll cut the gallery's commission in half as an anniversary gift to you and my brother, and you can have them for $3500."

Hanifa looked at Jahsani, who gave her his blessing. "I'll take'em!" she exclaimed, excited to purchase her first pieces of art. She chose the 3rd and 4th paintings.

Seven took out a red Sharpie and wrote SOLD and a number on the paintings' tags, then gave Hanifa a ticket so she could pay for them. His walkie-talkie started beeping.

"Go ahead," he spoke into it.

"It's time," responded the voice on the other end.

Looking at me, Seven replied, "I'm on my way." He removed the walkie-talkie from his mouth and said to us, "I gotta make the introduction, so get as close as y'all can."

"Okay. Good luck," I said then kissed him.

Kindred The Family Soul's *The Question* was playing, but the DJ cut it off as soon as Seven took the stage and grabbed the microphone.

"Ladies and gentlemen. Kings and queens. Can I have everyone's attention, please?"

The movement in the gallery came to a halt as the crowd directed their attention to the stage.

"I would like to thank everyone for coming out tonight to support all these amazingly talented artists who have shared their artistry with us.

"As always, I want to remind you that it's up to us to support and give value to art that reflects our culture and reality. Today's theme is Black Love. What is Black Love?" he asked, then paused.

"Black Love is many things at the same time. It's the foundation of all in existence, and it's woven into our being. Black Love is deeper than our fondness for a beautiful sister or handsome brother. It's unity, community, and the overall evolution of the human race.

"Black Love is timeless, boundless, and indestructible. It exists on every plane – celestial, metaphysical, and physical. It's been feared, demonized, portrayed by society as invaluable, yet it is the powerful element that sustained our ancestors through the most horrific travesty known to the human race in the great Maafa. "Black Love overcame slavery and thrived despite the spiritual and cultural severing by institutional racism, segregation, miseducation, mass-incarceration, marginalization of our
beautiful sisters, and yet it still exists because we exist!"

The crowd went into a frenzy of applause and whistles. Lights flashed from many cameras.

"The art on display embodies Black Love in the lives of everyday people, which all should appreciate. Before we move forward, I ask that you join me in welcoming to the stage my balance, my queen, and co-pilot of Black Love, Brooke." His smile was endless.

Shocked by his announcement, butterflies fluttered in my stomach like a baby was kicking to get out. People in the crowd were looking around for signs of movement, but my feet were glued to the floor.

"Go up there, Brooke," encouraged Hanifa and the others.

The crowd parted as I began to make my way to the stage. Seven helped me up the three steps and led me to the center of the stage. I was so nervous that all I could do was smile.

"A wise man once said that 'no nation can rise higher than its women. If there are no good women, there can be no good men.' This is my queen, and she is a phenomenal woman!"

The crowd went up in more applause and whistles.

"I love everything about this woman, and I want her to know that as we navigate through life together, I see you, value you, and will protect you and our family until my last breath."

I was doing all I could not to cry. My jaws hurt from smiling so hard.

"Although I'm proud to announce my love for you to the world," he said while pulling a sparkling, diamond ring out of his pocket, and getting down on one knee, "I would be more honored to tell the world you're my wife. Brooke Collins, will you marry me?"

"Yes! I'll marry you, baby!" I excitedly answered.

My mouth gaped open in astonishment as he placed the sevenkarat (four-karat solitaire stone atop) diamond ring on my finger. He stood up and we kissed to the cheers, applause, whistles, and flashing cameras of the crowd.

Hanifa, Michaela, and even women I didn't know were smiling and dabbing their eyes, trying to prevent their tears of joy from ruining their eyeliners.

Seven stood there with the biggest smile on his face.

"Kings and queens, Cultural Expressions proudly presents to you Black Love! Enjoy."

Chapter 14

(Michaela)

Nothing but blessings had rained down in the lives of me and my friends since the trip to Jamaica. Carl and I got engaged, our offer on the house was accepted, and my clients were satisfied with my services. Brooke learned that she was pregnant and got engaged to Seven. And Hanifa and Jahsani were preparing to celebrate ten years of marriage. Life was indeed good.

Carl was still asleep, so I slipped out of bed and went in the kitchen to turn on the coffee maker. I brought back a special blend I tried in Jamaica and had been drinking it every morning since. While waiting on it to brew, I opened my laptop and checked my emails. There were none, so I clicked on the blog to see what was going on. Surprisingly, Seven's Black Love showcase was the talk of the city. His speech and proposal were trending on social media. It hadn't been 24 hours and it was already at 20,000 views.

Carl and I were scheduled to close on the house tomorrow, so I clicked on the site of a couple local interior designers to see if I liked any of their previous work. This was going to be the home we planted our roots in, so I wanted it to be perfect for both of us.

I poured coffee into my mug. The rich taste awakened my senses as I scrolled down the screen. Two designers' work piqued my interest, so I took down their contact information and sent them an email.

It was Friday, and just because Brooke decided to stop working out, I didn't. I got myself together, put on my workout gear, and left Carl a note telling him I went to the gym and would be home afterwards.

Friday mornings at the gym were quiet and empty, except for the usual third-shift workers who came in before heading home. I stretched for a few minutes. It was cardio day, so my plan was to jog on the treadmill for forty-five minutes and then ride the bike for an equal length of time.

I put my earbuds in my ear, clicked on Pandora, sat my phone in the cup holder, adjusted the setting on the treadmill, and began jogging. Once I warmed up and broke a sweat, my mind wandered to a sensitive issue – children. This was something that frequently crossed my mind and had become even more frequent since Brooke announced she was pregnant.

For years, I'd lived with the regret of having an abortion my senior year in high school. I was young and had an opportunity to go to college, so at my mother's behest I went through with it. By the time I got on campus at Clarke, many of my friends were working on their second child and sinking into the trap of public housing and welfare. I'd had enough of both and decided not to have kids until I graduated and my career was intact.

I slipped up and got pregnant by Dee Dee my junior year but lost the baby due to a miscarriage. Carl and I talked about starting a family once we were sure our thing was more than a fling. *Seeing as how we're now engaged and just bought a house together, I think it's time we revisit that conversation.*

I was brought out of my reverie when the treadmill went into a five-minute cool down. Surprised that time had elapsed as fast as it had, I walked and squirted water in my mouth, then went and rode the bike.

When I walked through the door at home, Carl was sitting shirtless at the dining table eating two egg and cheese breakfast muffins and drinking a cup of coffee.

"Good morning, sleepy head," I kidded, sitting my gym bag on the floor and kissing his bald head.

"Morning, baby."

"Did you make me breakfast, too?"

His mouth was full, so he pointed to the stove where a cover was on a top of a plate to keep the eggs warm. I got two English muffins out the bag, dropped them in the toaster, then grabbed the orange juice out the refrigerator, and poured me a glass. The muffins popped up. I put grape jelly on them. I made two sandwiches and sat at the table with Carl.

"Did you get a good workout in?"

"Yeah. I had a lot on my mind, so I ran and then rode the bike." I bit into my sandwich.

"What's on your mind?" He took a sip of coffee.

I swallowed my food and washed it down with the juice. "For starters, now that we're closing on the house tomorrow, my focus is on us planning our wedding. I don't know if you want a big production or something more intimate."

His facial expression changed. "What kind of wedding do you want, Michaela?" he asked in a flat tone.

"Why you say it like that?"

"Like what? I simply asked what are your wedding expectations."

"I don't know. It's your wedding, too. You might want your folks from the country to come up and celebrate with us."

He took another bite of his sandwich and started talking with food in his mouth, which he knew was a pet-peeve of mine. "I say we grab a few of our friends, go down to the justice of peace, say our 'I Dos', then have a reception."

I looked at him like he was fourteen-karat crazy. "Quit playing with me, Carl."

"What's wrong with that? We'll be legally married, our friends and family can come kick it with us, and we'll save money," he said with a straight face.

"We ain't gotta do it big like Kim and Kanye but, damn, a shotgun wedding at the courthouse is not my ideal scenario. We can do better than that, Carl."

He finished the last bite of his sandwich, then sipped his coffee. "Michaela, I just bust my ass sixteen hours a day for ninety days straight so I could buy yo' ring and help with the down payment for the house. I don't have to have no big wedding. Anything intimate and feasible is ideal for me."

I understood where he was coming from, and the last thing I wanted was for him to work all that overtime again. The consultant in me instantly kicked in and I began thinking of solutions for a compromise.

"How about we do an island wedding? We can get married and have our honeymoon at the same time, then have a reception when we get back. I saw a brochure advertising that when we were at the resort. We don't have to go back to Jamaica; we can go somewhere else, like Hawaii or Antigua."

He thought it over as he sipped his coffee. "Are you sure you're cool with that?"

"Yes."

"Aight. Find something and let me know what it cost."

Smiling, I replied, "Okay." The power of compromise. "Also, I emailed a couple of interior designers, so we can pick one to help us decorate the house."

"I already told you, do whatever you want with the house, just leave the basement to me. I'm gon' put my furniture down there and turn it into my man cave," he said as he was getting up from the table.

"There's something else," I quickly added before he had time to go to the back.

"What's up?"

"I'm ready to start our family," I meekly stated.

"You ain't said nothin'. C'mon to the back and we can get it poppin' right now!" he said while humping the air, acting silly as if it was a joke.

With a stern facial expression, I retorted, "I'm serious, Carl."

Realizing I was serious, he stopped playing and leaned against the wall. "Okay, what you want me to do?"

"I'm just letting you know I won't be taking birth control anymore."

"Is that it?"

"That's it."

"Aight, now c'mon back here and let me play with all that ass!" He spanked the air as if it was my butt.

"Boy, I'm 'bout to put all this ass in the shower."

"You want some company?"

"Maybe," I replied with a seductive smirk on my face as I bit into the sandwich.

"Say less. I'm on my way."

I came up for air around one o'clock and went in the kitchen to get started packing. I went cabinet to cabinet taking things out, then wrapped up the dishes and put them in boxes. After finishing in the kitchen, I got started in the dining room. I removed the pictures off the walls and put the books into boxes.

As I was cleaning out the front closet, my phone started ringing. I maneuvered around several boxes and grabbed it off the dining table.

"Hello?"

"May I speak to Michaela?" asked an unfamiliar female voice.

"This is Michaela."

"Hi, Michaela. This is Bethany of Designs by Bethany. I got your email and wanted to give you a call about decorating your home."

"Okay. How are you doing?"

"I'm fine. Thanks for asking. Can you tell me a little bit about the style and look you're considering, how many rooms you would like decorated, and the budget you're working with?"

After filling Bethany in on the details of the house and our style and our budget, she agreed to come out to the house Sunday afternoon so we could collaborate on a design. Once we got off the phone, I finished packing up the front room, then went and got started in the bedroom.

Due to anxiety, I tossed and turned all night. I thought about how far I'd come and all I'd accomplished, but still felt uneasy. Who would have thought a chick from the projects would graduate college, quit a job at a Fortune 500 company, start my own business, and get engaged to a wonderful man with whom I was buying my first home? Correction: our first home.

Today's forecast said it was going to be sunny and hot. Carl and I planned to go have lunch and celebrate after closing on the house, so after getting out of the shower I did a quick beat. I cleansed and moisturized my face, added a little primer, stroked on some foundation and concealer. I put on mascara and eyeliner, then a yellow maxi-dress and sandals.

The energy and excitement of owning our own home was etched on both of our faces as Carl's Escalade cruised along 285.

"You ready, baby?" he asked with a smile.

"I am! To be on the cusp of fulfilling one of my childhood dreams feels like a dream."

"I hear you. I'm excited because our journey together has begun."

I knew it was real once he turned onto our street. Our realtor's, Terrese, blue Jaguar truck was parked in front of the house. Carl pulled in the driveway and parked. Terrese greeted us at the door, jingling the keys in her hand. "Today's the big day!" she said smiling.

We followed her inside to the kitchen, where she had three forms laid out on the island counter for us to sign. Carl reached into his pocket and pulled out a green, rectangular box with a gold lace tied around it. He handed it to me.

"What's this?" I asked as I untied and opened the case. It was a green and gold cross-pen.

"With this pen our family will record all our special occasions, like buying this house, our marriage license, and our children's birth certificates. It'll be passed down from generation to generation as a family heirloom," he said, looking at me with loving eyes.

The pen enriched the special moment. I took it out the case and signed my name on the documents. He signed his name afterwards.

"Congratulations! You two are the owners of this beautiful home!" cheered Terrese as she handed me the keys. She gathered the papers and headed for the door.

As soon as I heard the door close, I screamed and did a little dance. "We did it! We did it!" Overwhelmed with excitement,

Carl gave me a big hug and kiss. We walked through every square inch of the house envisioning ourselves living here. The last room we toured was the master suite. It was a blank canvas waiting on our special touch. I walked in the bathroom and looked around. Carl was in the doorway grinning like a Cheshire cat when I turned around.

"What?" I asked, curious to know why he was grinning.

"It's only one thing left to do." He walked towards me.

"What's that?" I asked as he wrapped his arms around me in a loving embrace, then squeezed my soft backside.

"We gotta christen our new house."

The sensual contact and sparkle in his pretty eyes made it difficult to resist, so I succumbed to his charm. We celebrated right there on the bathroom counter. But wait! Not only there. We also did it on the bedroom floor and in front of the mirror in the walk-in closet. *Welcome Home!*

Chapter 15

(Hanifa)

I felt a sense of excitement from the moment my eyes opened this morning. Today marks our tenth year of being married. The mild milestone wasn't without its fair share of trials and tribulations, but through it all we remained committed and supportive of one another.

To start the morning off right, I woke Jahsani up with a tantalizing performance of fellatio. My thinking was to set the tone for the next ten years by keeping it spicy, spontaneous, and satisfying.

My parents were staying in the guest room down the hall next to the kids' bedroom. Because it was so quiet in the house, I covered my face with a pillow to muffle the moans of pleasure while Jahsani licked and stroked me to multiple orgasms.

Our anniversary cookout was arranged by one of Michaela's event planning contacts. Her team came out yesterday to string up lights, and today they're scheduled to set up the tables and dance floor in the back yard. Jahsani's uncle was set to start grilling at noon. That way, by 5:30pm it wouldn't be too smoggy when people began arriving. Several of my family members from California and Chicago flew in to celebrate with us. We expected close to 50 people and a DJ, who was to perform until 11pm, so I gave my neighbors a heads-up and invited them to come get a plate or a drink if they'd like.

Me and my mother shared a joint while surveying the garden as uncle Johnny got the grill going.

"Lookie here," she said, eyeing my greens, "someone finally learned to use the right compost," she teased.

"You were right, mom," I admitted.

Brooke and Michaela walked out the kitchen door. They were the daughters my parents never had, and they loved when my parents visited.

"Momma Asante!"

"There go my babies!" replied my mother with joy as they hugged. "Congratulations, ladies! I hear two kings are ready to make honest women out of you two," she teased.

"Thanks, mom," said Michaela. "It's so good to see you!"

"And you as well. When will I get to meet these guys?"

"Today," answered Brooke. "He'll be with me when I come back. I just came by to drop off the pans of macaroni and cheese Seven made. Make sure you get some because it's the bomb!"

"Umm, ain't nothing like a man that can cook in the kitchen and the bedroom," she brazenly stated.

"Ain't that the truth!" agreed Brooke.

"I understand you're carrying a glorious one."

"I am," replied Brooke, smiling and rubbing her stomach.

My mother placed her hand on top of Brooke's. "Blessed is the fruit of thy womb, my child." She then looked at Michaela. "And when are you gonna give me some grandbabies, beautiful?"

"Soon, momma. Soon!"

"Well, aight. Let me go in here and check on him. By now he done probably turned them kids into revolutionaries," my mother joked. "See you later, ladies!"

"Bye, mom," said Brooke and Michaela simultaneously.

We were quiet for a brief moment. We stood there smiling as we watched my mother walk away.

"It looks nice back here, 'Nifa," complimented Brooke.

"Yeah, Michaela's people hooked it up. The DJ will be here by 5, so we gonna have a good time tonight."

"Do you need anything else?" asked Michaela.

"No, I just wanna thank you two for everything. Since the day we met, y'all been my sisters. I love y'all." I hugged them both.

"We love you, too!"

I walked them down the driveway to their cars. "See y'all later."

"Peace."

As soon as I went back to the house and opened the door, I saw Jahlil and Jahlissa standing front and center with their hands behind their backs. They were reciting the Black Panther Party's

Ten-Point Program with my father. It brought back childhood memories because I was their age when he drilled it into me. They were on the third point when my father looked up at me.

"Watch this, kids. Front and center, Hanifa!" he authoritatively commanded.

Ten years of training and discipline kicked in. I hurriedly stood beside the kids with my hands behind my back.

"Recite points four and five, queen," he commanded.

"We want decent housing, fit for shelter of human beings. Five, we want education for our people that exposes the true nature of this decadent American society. We want education that teaches us our true history and role in the present-day society."

It had been 15 years since I'd been asked to recite any of the Ten-Point Program, but I was raised to live by them, so recalling them wasn't hard.

"See, I told you she knew them by heart. I'm gon' Zoom call y'all every week, and we are going to go over them so that both of y'all know them, too. So, you better study and memorize them," he instructed the kids then gave me that look. "It's time, baby."

"Yes, sir," I replied. I knew exactly what he meant.

My father believed every black child should know the Ten-Point Program and be taught our culture and history because the school system is designed to deprogram our collective consciousness and to indoctrinate us into hating ourselves and accepting an inferior societal role. Connection to one's culture and history builds self-esteem and confidence in a child, so when they encounter kids from different cultures they won't feel less than.

Growing up with freedom fighters as parents was a blessing. I looked forward to teaching and sharing with my children all the things that were taught and given to me.

The afternoon was slowly waning, so I took a shower and got dressed. I put on the red dashiki dress my mother made me, and some black sandals. Jahsani had trimmed my loose ends yesterday, so I picked out my afro until it was a symmetrical sphere, then sprayed it with oil sheen. Jahsani had on black shorts and the red dashiki shirt my mother had made for him; he also wore black sandals. I had braided his locs after he cut my ends, so they looked stylish.

By 4:30pm, the aroma of burnt hickory wood, barbecue, and tangy marinades filled the air. Our house was filled with my cousins, their kids, and some of Jahsani's family. DJ Supreme was in the backyard setting his equipment up. Uncle Johnny was putting the finishing touches on the ribs. My father was icing down the beer and soda bins.

As soon as the soulful sound of Teddy Pendergrass' *Love T.K.O.* came on, people slowly trickled into the backyard and began the festivities. A couple of my cousins started a game of corn hole in the driveway, and some played spades in the backyard. Shortly thereafter, my mother-in-law and Uncle Johnny's wife brought the food out the house and sat it up on the picnic table. The celebration was officially underway.

Being surrounded by so many familiar faces felt like a mini family reunion. This was clearly the right way to celebrate our anniversary. Jahsani seemed happy as well. He was enjoying a beer and talking with several of his friends and cousins when I approached.

"Hi, everyone," I said to all. To Jahsani, asked, "What you want on your plate, baby?"

"Some wings, a couple of ribs, baked beans, potato salad, and some macaroni and cheese."

I walked over to the food and my mother and I were making our husbands' plates when Brooke and Seven entered the backyard.

"Y'all just in time," I said to them.

"Happy anniversary, Hanifa," said Seven with a soft kiss on the cheek.

"Thanks, Seven."

Brooke was all smiles. "Momma Asante, this is my fiancé, Seven. Seven, this is Hanifa's mother, Momma Asante."

Seven bowed his head. "It's an honor to meet you, queen mother."

"Peace and blessings, king," she replied, reading his energy. "Now, this is the man for you, Brooke," she said with conviction.

I took Jahsani his plate then walked Brooke and Seven over to where my father was sitting in the shade.

"Papa D, this is my fiancé, Seven. Seven, this is Hanifa's father, Mr. Olu Dara."

Seven extended his hand. "I'm honored to meet you, king."

"Likewise, king," my father replied, still holding onto Seven's hand. "This is one of my daughters, and I am extremely protective of them. Can I trust you to love and protect her, Seven?"

"Absolutely, king."

"My man," my father replied, then released Seven's hand.

At that very moment, Michaela and Carl walked into the backyard. Guys began rubber-necking like they never saw a beautiful woman.

My father's face lit up with excitement when he saw her.

"Hey there, trouble-maker!"

"What's up, Papa D" you looking real good these days," Michaela flirted as she hugged and kissed him on the cheek. "Papa D, Momma Asante, this is my soon to be husband, Carl. Carl, these are my other parents."

"It's nice to meet both of you."

I could tell by the look on my mother's face that she was reading his energy. "It's nice to meet you, too."

My father shook Carl's hand. "That's a good grip you got, son. It's good to see you're in shape 'cause you got ya hands full with that one," he joked with Carl. "I'm gon' tell you like I just told Seven. This is my daughter and I'm extremely protective of her. Can I trust you to love and protect her, Carl?"

"Yes, sir, you can," answered Carl. He looked my father directly in the eyes the whole time.

Once the sun dropped below the horizon, the effects of the Crown Royal, Hennessy, Ciroc, and wine kicked in. Aunts, uncles, friends, and grandparents were out on the dance floor having a good time. Watching my parents dance to Stevie Wonder's *These Three Words* warmed my heart. I prayed my marriage lasted as long as theirs.

The volume of the music suddenly dropped. Brooke got the microphone from the DJ.

"Can I have everyone's attention for a moment. I just wanna acknowledge my sister and brother and say happy ten-year anniversary! Watching you two grow over the years has been a blessing and testament that true love still exists. I wish you both many more years of good health, love, and prosperity. I love you!"

She handed the mic back to the DJ, who also had something to say.

"It's customary that the married couple say a few words, so come on up Hanifa and Jahsani."

Jahsani led me from the dance floor over to the DJ stand. He got the microphone and passed it to me.

"I didn't plan on speaking tonight, so I'll try and keep it short. I wanna thank all of you for being here to celebrate our ten-year anniversary with us. I give thanks to the Creator for my parents, who gave me life. To my mother, I'm forever thankful for the example you set for how a strong, black woman carries herself, treats others, and takes care of her family. Because of you, I've become the woman, mother, and wife I am today.

"To my father, you are my cheat sheet. I'm thankful for everything you've taught me. You showed me what a real man is, what love looks like, feels like, and that is what allowed me to recognize this amazing man I married ten years ago. Growing up, you bolstered my self-confidence by telling me I was beautiful, and not just for a dark-skinned girl, but because I am divine. You taught me I could achieve anything I set my mind to... and I have. I love you, daddy!" I cried out like a little girl, blowing him a kiss.

I turned and faced Jahsani. "To my king... my best friend... my rock. Baby, I'm so thankful for having such a selfless, humble, hardworking, and loving man like you as a husband. You're an amazing father, and I look forward to loving you for the rest of my life. I love you." I kissed him and then handed him the mic.

"Wow... how do you follow that?" he asked with an incredulous smile. "To our family, thank you for all the love and support you have given us over the years, for allowing us to make mistakes and figure it out on our own, for helping with the twins so we could go on a date, and for showing up for their birthdays. We couldn't celebrate ten years of marriage without y'all's help."

He turned and faced me. He held my hand and looked deep into my eyes. "To my queen... my best friend... my balance. Baby, I am the luckiest man in the world because of you. Loving and being loved by you are the highlights of my life. You've given me two beautiful children. You've made our house into a home. You have been the biggest supporter of every idea I had or dream I wanted to pursue.

"When we first got together, I told you whether it's this lifetime or the next, my spirit wouldn't be at peace until we were together.

I meant it then and I mean it now. All I ask of you is that you outlive me so that I never have to experience a day of living without you. I love you!"

DJ Supreme cut the music back up, and we danced the night away.

The Presence and Power of Black Love is Eternal!

Made in the USA
Columbia, SC
15 September 2021

45555098R00143